Joseph Dalton Hooker, Asa Gray

# The Vegetation of the Rocky Mountain Region

and a comparison with that of other parts of the world

Joseph Dalton Hooker, Asa Gray

**The Vegetation of the Rocky Mountain Region**
*and a comparison with that of other parts of the world*

ISBN/EAN: 9783337381721

Printed in Europe, USA, Canada, Australia, Japan

Cover: Foto ©Andreas Hilbeck / pixelio.de

More available books at **www.hansebooks.com**

DEPARTMENT OF THE INTERIOR.
UNITED STATES GEOLOGICAL AND GEOGRAPHICAL SURVEY.
F. V. HAYDEN, U. S. Geologist-in-Charge.

# THE VEGETATION

OF THE

# ROCKY MOUNTAIN REGION,

AND

## A COMPARISON WITH THAT OF OTHER PARTS OF THE WORLD.

BY

**ASA GRAY and SIR J. D. HOOKER, F, R. S.**

— —

EXTRACTED FROM THE BULLETIN OF THE SURVEY, VOL. VI, No. 1.

WASHINGTON, February 11, 1881.

# BULLETIN

OF THE

## UNITED STATES GEOLOGICAL AND GEOGRAPHICAL SURVEY OF THE TERRITORIES.

VOLUME VI. 1880. NUMBER 1.

## Art. I.—The Vegetation of the Rocky Mountain Region and a Comparison with that of other Parts of the World.

### By Asa Gray and Joseph D. Hooker.

I.

### THE VEGETATION OF THE ROCKY MOUNTAIN REGION.

The vegetation of the wide central tract which lies between the Atlantic United States and those which border on the Pacific is replete with interest and importance, both scientific and economical. We are to sketch its general features, as made known to us by personal observation, by the published observations of others, and by the botanical studies to which we have been devoted. For doing this to much purpose, it is necessary to compare or to contrast the vegetation of the district in question with that of the more fertile regions on both sides, and with a somewhat similar wide interior district in another part of the northern temperate zone.

By "the Atlantic States," as contradistinguished from those of the Pacific, we here mean not only those which touch upon the Atlantic Ocean, but also those which border the Mississippi River, on its western as well as its eastern side; the great woodless plains being taken as their western limit. The term "Rocky Mountain Region," here used in its widest sense, and in the lack of a better appellation, we propose to apply in general in such wise as to include the gradually elevated plateau which flanks the eastern base of the Rocky Mountains on the one hand, and the equally elevated district or plateau, thickly traversed by mountain ranges, which extends westward to the eastern base of the Sierra Nevada of California, and the Cascade Mountains further north. As to the Rocky Mountains themselves, it is most convenient and natural, from our point of view, to comprise under this general designation all the ranges as far west as the Wahsatch inclusive.

We understand the term *Cordilleras*, brought into use by Professor

1 G B

Whitney, to be a comprehensive appellation for the whole system of mountains, from the most eastern Rocky Mountains to the Sierra Nevada inclusive, and the continuation of the latter in the Cascade Mountains of Oregon and British Columbia. The region which we are to treat botanically might take the name of the Cordilleran Region of North America. But it will, on several accounts, be better to adhere in this essay to the designation used in our title. For, although the term "cordilleras" would be the only appropriate one if we had the whole vast mountain system in view, from Patagonia to the Arctic sea-coast, it is a term which belongs primarily and mainly to South America, and our survey is to embrace only a few parallels of latitude, in fact just those which contain the ranges which early took the name of the Rocky Mountains, both at the north, where they were traversed by Lewis and Clarke at the beginning of this century (1803–1806), and at the south, where they were reached on the frontiers of New Mexico by Pike a year or two later.

With these Rocky Mountains proper, i. e. the eastern and dominating ranges, as the central line of our field of view, the horizon should extend eastward to where the gradually subsiding plain becomes green with a rich prairie vegetation, to be at length fringed with forest, and westward to the base of the Sierra Nevada and the Cascades, the eastern verge of the Pacific forest region.

In a developed treatise, the physical geography and the climatic elements of the region would have to pass under review, and the multifarious and scattered botanical data would have to be collected, discussed, and tabulated. We cannot undertake an exhaustive task like this, nor could we add much to what has already been done in various well-considered and well-known government reports. The climatology and the practical considerations deducible from it form the subject of Major Powell's " Report on the Lands of the Arid Region of the United States," the second edition of which was issued in 1879. In the "General Report" which forms the introduction to the botanical volume of Clarence King's celebrated "Survey on the Fortieth Parallel" (and which prefaces that elaborate systematic treatise which was too modestly styled a "Catalogue," and so has by some been cited as such), Mr. Sereno Watson has thoroughly and ably discussed the elements of the flora of the Great Basin, exemplifying it with lists and other details. And for a district further south, Professor Rothrock, in his volume on the Botany of Wheeler's Surveys, has within the last year published his instructive notes on the characteristic features of the botany of Colorado, New Mexico, and a part of Arizona. Professor Sargent has given a useful sketch of the arboreal and frutescent vegetation of Nevada in the American Journal of Science for June, 1879; and among Professor Hayden's very important reports, that of Henry Gannett, " On the Arable and Pasture Lands of Colorado" (1875, reprinted in 1878), is noteworthy.

Our sketch must be, like our observations, a rapid and cursory reconnaissance, noting some features which arrested our attention, drawing some comparisons, and suggesting inferences which seem to us probable.

The phytogeography of the temperate portion of the North American continent, in broad outlines is evidently this: An Atlantic forest region; a Pacific forest region; and, between the two, the wide interior, mainly non-forest, region—the special subject of our essay; a region not easy to name nor to describe succinctly, but of which the eastern half is a vast woodless plain, gradually and evenly rising, so that its western margin is about 5,000 feet above the sea-level; then a mountain belt, the highest ridges and peaks of which rise from 11,000 to 14,400 feet; then, shut out from moisture by these mountains on the east and the Sierra on the west, an arid interior district of plains, at an average of 5,000 feet above the sea. This is mainly desert, and is traversed by many mountain ranges, generally of north and south direction, and reaching an elevation of 9,000 or 10,000 feet, or rarely higher. This whole interior, of miles average breadth—like other great interiors not very exceptionally favored—is marked by the scantiness or absence of arboreal vegetation and of rainfall, the former being in great measure dependent on the latter. Its plains are treeless except along water-courses; the mountains bear trees along sheltered ravines and on their higher slopes, upon which there is considerable condensation of moisture; but, whenever they rise to a certain height (about 11,000 feet in latitude 37° to 41°), they are woodless from cold and other hardship attending elevation, although they enjoy an abundant condensation of moisture, mostly in the form of snow.

The Rocky Mountain region may be therefore divided vertically into three botanical districts:

1. An arid and woodless district, which occupies far the greater part of the area.

2. A wooded district, in some places covering, in others locally adorning, the mountain slopes.

3. An alpine unwooded district above the belt where trees exist. But in some places, slopes woodless from dryness merge into tracts woodless from cold, no proper forest belt intervening.

These three botanical districts may be separately investigated.

The smallest in area—since it is restricted to mountain summits and the least peculiar, is—

## I.—THE ALPINE REGION.

Botanically the alpine regions of the temperate zone in the northern hemisphere are southward prolongations of arctic vegetation, almost pure in the boreal parts, but more and more mixed with special types in lower latitudes, these special types being a part of the flora which is characteristic of each continent in those latitudes.

Leaving out of view a considerable number of temperate species which here and there become alpestrine or persist in dwarfed forms within some truly alpine regions, the alpine flora of the United States does not comprise a large number of species. It may be useful to present a tabulated list of them, i. e., of the phænogamous portion, under three heads, placing the ampler Rocky Mountain alpine flora in the center and the more restricted Atlantic and Pacific alpine floras one on each side.

It will be understood that the survey is limited to the United States proper, reaching latitude 47° on the Atlantic and 49° 40' on the Pacific side, in all of which the proper alpine flora is confined to high altitudes, from about 5,000 to over 14,000 feet above the sea-level. On the Atlantic side it is only a matter of a few isolated summits in New England and Northern New York, the Alleghanian or Apalachian chain and its dependencies not being high enough in New York and Pennsylvania, and being in too low latitude notwithstanding their greater elevation in the Carolinas, to have more than alpestrine vegetation, although a few properly alpine species linger on the summits. On the Pacific side we have to do only with the Sierra Nevada and its northern prolongation; and there, too, we make latitude 47° the northern limit, because north of that parallel, we cannot at present well determine the limit between what belongs to the Rocky Mountains and what to the continuation of the Cascade Mountains.

The species which are not arctic are distinguished by italic type; when the genera are peculiar to the region, the generic name is printed in small capitals. To save space in the columns, the names are printed without reference to authorship.

The left-hand column is so insignificant, that it might have been omitted. We cannot amplify it by adding alpine plants from farther north, such as the stragglers about the Gulf of Saint Lawrence and the Labrador flora, for these are found nearly at the sea-level and are extensions of the proper arctic flora.

| Atlantic United States Alpine. | Rocky Mountain Alpine. | Pacific United States Alpine. |
|---|---|---|
| | Thalictrum alpinum. Anemone narcissiflora. | Anemone narcissiflora. *Anemone occidentalis* (A. Baldensis Hook). |
| | *Ranunculus Eschscholtzii.* Ranunculus pygmæus. *Ranunculus adoneus.* *Ranunculus Macauleyi.* | *Ranunculus Eschscholtzii.* Ranunculus pygmæus. |
| | | *Ranunculus oxynotus.* |
| | Papaver alpinum (nudicaule). Parrya macrocarpa. Cardamine bellidifolia. *Draba aurea.* Draba alpina. Draba hirta or arctica. *Draba crassifolia.* Draba stellata or muricella. *Draba rentosa.* | Papaver alpinum (nudicaule). Parrya macrocarpa. Cardamine bellidifolia. *Draba aurea.* Draba alpina. |
| Cardamine bellidifolia. | | *Draba crassifolia.* Draba stellata or muricella. *Draba eurycarpa.* *Draba Douglasii.* Draba ...... |

| Atlantic United States Alpine. | Rocky Mountain Alpine. | Pacific United States Alpine. |
|---|---|---|
| | Smelowskia calycina. | Smelowskia calycina. |
| | Thlaspi alpestro. | Thlaspi alpestro. |
| | *Lychnis (Melandrium) Kingii.* | |
| | | *Lychnis (Mel.) Californica.* |
| Silene acaulis. | Silene acaulis. | Silene acaulis. |
| | Cerastium alpinum. | Cerastium alpinum. |
| *Arenaria Grœnlandica.* | | |
| Arenaria verna or vars. | Arenaria verna or vars. | Arenaria verna or vars. |
| | Arenaria Rossii. | |
| | Arenaria biflora. | Arenaria biflora. |
| | Arenaria arctica. | Arenaria arctica. |
| | Sagina nivalis. | |
| | *Claytonia arctica, megarrhiza.* | |
| | Calandrinia pygmæa. | *Calandrinia pygmæa.* |
| | *Trifolium nanum.* | |
| | Trifolium andinum. | |
| | *Trifolium dasyphyllum.* | |
| | Trifolium Parryi. | |
| | *Astragalus calycosus.* | |
| Astragalus alpinus. | Astragalus alpinus. | Astragalus alpinus. |
| | Oxytropis podocarpa. | |
| | Oxytropis Uralensis, arctica. | |
| | Oxytropis nana. | |
| | Oxytropis multiceps | |
| | | Eriogynia pectinata. |
| Rubus Chamæmorus. | Rubus Chamæmorus. | |
| | Rubus arcticus. | Rubus arcticus. |
| Dryas octopetala ! | Dryas octopetala and var. | Dryas octopetala. |
| | *Geum Rossii.* | |
| *Geum radiatum, Peckii.* | | |
| Potentilla frigida. | Potentilla frigida? | |
| | | *Potentilla gelida.* |
| | | Potentilla Breweri. |
| | *Potentilla diversifolia.* | *Potentilla diversifolia.* |
| | *Potentilla nivea.* | |
| | | *Potentilla villosa.* |
| | IVESIA *Gordoni* | IVESIA *Gordoni.* |
| | | IVESIA *Muiri.* |
| Sibbaldia procumbens. | Sibbaldia procumbens. | Sibbaldia procumbens. |
| | Saxifraga adscendens. | |
| | *Saxifraga Jamesii.* | |
| Saxifraga rivularis. | Saxifraga rivularis. | Saxifraga rivularis. |
| | *Saxifraga debilis.* | |
| | Saxifraga cernua. | Saxifraga cernua. |
| | Saxifraga Hirculus. | |
| | *Saxifraga chrysantha.* | |
| | | *Saxifraga Tolmiei.* |
| Saxifraga stellaris. | Saxifraga stellaris | Saxifraga stellaris. |
| | | *Saxifraga bryophora.* |
| | Saxifraga punctata | Saxifraga punctata. |
| | Saxifraga Dahurica. | Saxifraga Dahurica. |
| | Saxifraga nivalis. | Saxifraga nivalis. |
| | Saxifraga cæspitosa. | Saxifraga cæspitosa. |
| | Saxifraga bronchialis. | Saxifraga bronchialis. |
| | Saxifraga teiospitata. | |
| | Saxifraga flagellaris. | Saxifraga flagellaris. |
| Saxifraga oppositifolia. | Saxifraga oppositifolia. | Saxifraga oppositifolia. |
| | Chrysosplenium alternifolium. | Chrysosplenium alternifolium. |
| Sedum Rhodiola. | Sedum Rhodiola. | Sedum Rhodiola. |
| | *Sedum rhodanthum.* | |
| | Epilobium latifolium. | Epilobium latifolium. |
| | | *Epilobium chordatum.* |
| | CYMOPTERUS *alpinus* | |
| | CYMOPTERUS *humilis* | CYMOPTERUS cinerascens. |
| | | CYMOPTERUS Necadensis. |
| | APLOPAPPUS *pygmæus.* | |
| | APLOPAPPUS *Lyallii.* | Aplopappus Lyallii |
| Solidago humilis, var. alpina. | Solidago humilis, var. alpina. | |
| | TOWNSENDIA *cœlonaata.* | |
| | TOWNSENDIA *Rothrockii.* | |
| | Aster audibus | |
| | Aster alpinus | |
| | | Erigeron compositum. |
| (Grœnland.) | Erigeron uniflorum. | Erig ron uniflorum |
| | *Erigeron grandiflorum* | |
| | *Erigeron uniosum* | *Erigeron ursinum.* |
| | *Erigeron radiatum* | |
| | Antennaria alpina | Antennaria alpina. |
| Gnaphalium supinum | | |
| | ACTINELLA *acaulifera.* | |
| | ACTINELLA *Brandegea* | |
| | HYMENOXYS *alpin?* | |
| | HYMENOXYS *nana* | |

| Atlantic United States Alpine. | Rocky Mountain Alpine. | Pacific United States Alpine. |
|---|---|---|
| Artemisia borealis, L. Sup. | Artemisia borealis. *Artemisia scopulorum.* Artemisia arctica. *Senecio Fremonti.* *Senecio amplectens.* *Senecio Soldanella.* Crepis nana. *Hieracium triste.* | Artemisia arctica. *Senecio Fremonti.* Crepis nana. *Hieracium triste.* |
| Nabalus *nanus.* Nabalus *Boottii.* | Taraxacum lævigatum. Campanula uniflora. *Vaccinium cæspitosum.* Arctostaphylos alpina. | *Vaccinium cæspitosum.* |
| *Vaccinium cæspitosum.* Arctostaphylos alpina. Cassiope hypnoides. | Cassiope tetragona. *Cassiope Mertensiana.* | Cassiope tetragona. *Cassiope Mertensiana.* *Cassiope lycopodioides.* *Bryanthus Breweri.* *Bryanthus empetriformis.* |
| Bryanthus taxifolius. | *Bryanthus empetriformis.* *Bryanthus glanduliflorus.* Rhododendron Lapponicum. | *Bryanthus glanduliflorus.* |
| Rhododendron Lapponicum. Loiseleuria procumbens. Diapensia Lapponica. | | |
| | *Primula angustifolia.* *Primula Parryi.* | *Primula angustifolia.* *Primula suffrutescens.* |
| | *Douglasia nivalis.* *Douglasia montana.* Androsace Chamæjasme. *Gentiana barbellata.* Gentiana tenella. *Gentiana propinqua.* *Gentiana arctophila.* Gentiana prostrata. Gentiana glauca. Gentiana frigida. | Androsace Chamæjasme. |
| | | *Gentiana Newberryi.* |
| | *Gentiana Parryi.* *Phlox bryoides.* *Phlox muscoides.* *Phlox cæspitosa.* Gilia *Brandegei.* *Polemonium confertum.* *Polemonium viscosum.* Polemonium humile. Eritrichium nanum. *Mertensia alpina.* Chionophila *Jamesii.* Synthyris *alpina.* | *Phlox cæspitosa.* *Polemonium confertum.* Polemonium humile. Eritrichium nanum. |
| Veronica alpina. Castilleia pallida, var sept. | Veronica alpina. Castilleia pallida, var. sept. *Castilleia breviflora.* | Veronica alpina. Castilleia pallida, var. |
| Euphrasia officinalis (gracilis). | Euphrasia officinalis (gracilis). *Pedicularis Grœnlandica.* *Pedicularis Parryi.* | *Pedicularis Grœnlandica.* |
| | | *Pedicularis ornithorrhyncha.* |
| | *Pedicularis scopulorum.* Pedicularis flammea. *Paronychia pulvinata.* *Eriogonum androsaceum.* | |
| | | *Eriogonum incanum.* *Eriogonum Lobbii.* *Eriogonum pyrolæfolium.* |
| | *Eriogonum Kingii.* Koenigia Islandica. Oxyria digyna. | |
| Oxyria digyna. | | Oxyria digyna. *Polygonum Shastense.* |
| Polygonum viviparum. | Polygonum viviparum. *Polygonum minimum.* Salix arctica, var. Salix reticulata. *Salix phlelophylla.* | Polygonum viviparum. Salix arctica, var. Salix reticulata. *Salix phlelophylla.* |
| Salix herbacea. Salix Uva-Ursi ? Empetrum nigrum. *Habenaria obtusata.* | *Habenaria obtusata.* Tofieldia palustris. *Tofieldia coccinea.* Lloydia serotina. Luzula spicata. Luzula arcuata. | |
| Luzula spicata. Luzula arcuata. | | Lloydia serotina. Luzula spicata. Luzula arcuata. |

| Atlantic United States Alpine. | Rocky Mountain Alpine. | Pacific United States Alpine. |
|---|---|---|
| Juncus trifidus. | Juncus triglumis. Juncus biglumis. Juncus Parryi. Juncus Drummondi. Juncus castaneus. | Juncus Parryi. Juncus Drummondii. Juncus castaneus. Juncus chlorocephalus. |
| | Kobresia scirpina. Kobresia caricina. Carex Pyrenaica. Carex nigricans. | Carex Pyrenaica. Carex nigricans. |
| Carex scirpoidea. | Carex scirpoidea. Carex obtusata. Carex Lyoni. | Carex scirpoidea. |
| Carex capitata. | Carex capitata. | |
| | Carex incurva. | Carex Broweri. |
| Carex atrata. Carex alpina. | Carex atrata. Carex alpina. Carex fuliginosa. Carex frigida. Carex fœtida. Carex lagopina. | Carex atrata. Carex fœtida. Carex lagopina. |
| Carex rigida. Carex rariflora. | Carex rigida. Carex rariflora. Carex podocarpa. | |
| Carex capillaris. | Carex capillaris. Carex filifolia. Carex concinna. | Carex podocarpa. Carex filifolia. Carex luzulæfolia. |
| Phleum alpinum. | Alopecurus alpinus. Phleum alpinum. Agrostis rubra. etc. | Phleum alpinum. |
| Calamagrostis Pickeringii. Hierochloa alpina. Trisetum subspicatum. Aivra atropurpurea. Poa laxa. | Hierochloa alpina. Trisetum subspicatum. Poa laxa. Poa arctica. | Trisetum subspicatum. |
| Poa alpina. | Poa alpina. Festuca brevifolia or rubra. | Poa alpina. Festuca brevifolia or rubra. |
| 52 sp. | 184 sp. | 111 sp. |

The analysis of this alpine flora need not detain us. The botanist sees at a glance that it is the arctic flora, or rather prolongations of it, extended southward along the mountains of sufficient elevation, with certain admixtures of types pertaining to the vegetation of the regions.

The peculiar elements in the scanty alpine flora of the Eastern United States are only five species, viz: One grass of arctic affinity, *Calamagrostis Pickeringii*; an orchid, *Habenaria obtusata*; a *Geum*, which has its principal home on the subalpine summits of the Alleghanies farther south, and is nearly represented by a species on the Northern Pacific coast; and two species of *Nabalus*, which will be allowed to be altered states of species peculiar to North America and nearly peculiar to the Atlantic side.

The Pacific alpine flora has a higher proportional number of non-arctic species, as must needs be, considering its long stretch through so many parallels of latitude; but the number pertaining to non-arctic genera is small. They are—

*Calandrinia pygmæa.*  
*Eriogynia pectinata.*  
*Ivesia*, 2 species.  
*Cymopterus*, 2 species.  
*Aplopappus Lyallii.*  
*Eriogonum*, 3 species.

All of them are of genera peculiar to America. Besides these, only 38 species are peculiar to America, and between a third and a quarter of these are known to extend to Arctic America. Of the whole 111 species about 50 are not known in Europe and Asia in identical species.

The list of Rocky Mountain alpine species reaches the number of 184.

Those of the Sierra in California, and northward up to the British boundary, to 111.

Those of the mountains in the northeastern part of the Atlantic States (the Alleghanies, though reaching a greater altitude, are not high enough for the latitude to have any alpine vegetation, though they verge on it) are only 52.

The comparative meagerness of this last list is not surprising when we consider how very restricted the alpine area altogether is in Maine, New Hampshire (which has most of it), and the northeastern corner of New York. And we have not taken into account the arctic-alpine species which descend to the sea-level on the shores of the Gulf of Saint Lawrence, nor the few which occur on the bleak northern shore of Lake Superior. The latter, as some one has well suggested, owe their existence or continuance there neither to the absolute elevation nor to the latitude, but to the moist bleakness of a wind-swept coast, which gives them congenial summer conditions, on ground which forest cannot stand upon, owing to the severe exposure. Yet this forest resumes its sway northward, as soon as some shelter is given.

The Pacific alpine region, notwithstanding its long stretch along the mountain tops of a continuous but narrow north and south range, is also a restricted one. In California only the very culminations of the Sierra Nevada can be said to be alpine, and they are too arid in summer for the development of a true alpine flora. In Oregon and Washington Territory there is equal height under more northern parallels of latitude, abiding snow, and summer rain. The botany of these heights is far from well known. Probably all the arctic species of the Rocky Mountain column also belong there, and a fair share of exclusive species.

It is difficult to say what are or are not alpine species in the Sierra Nevada, especially southward, where, notwithstanding the heavy winter fall of snow, the higher elevations are unwooded from dryness as much as from cold. But, as we have excluded species which show themselves to be at home at lower altitudes, and have included all arctic-alpine types, the number of questionable character is very small.

Nor, except that we know their ranges and aptitudes better, is there much less difficulty in drawing a line between truly alpine and alpestrine species in the other regions. There are a goodly number of species which are normal to low altitudes or to the sea-level in the northern temperate zone, such as *Campanula rotundifolia, Taraxacum Dens-leonis, Androsace septentrionalis, Eriophorum alpinum, polystachyon,* &c., and *Festuca ovina*, which also flourish in an alpine station. And, indeed, these same species, and others like them (such as *Erigeron compositum*, which flourishes at the base as well as on the highest summits of the Rocky Mountains, and also in Greenland), make a part of the extreme arctic flora. Any list will therefore be to some extent arbitrary. For example, in the Atlantic alpine list, while *Cardamine bellidifolia*, *Silene acaulis*, *Sibbaldia procumbens*, *Gnaphalium supinum*, *Rhododendron Lapponicum*, *Diapensia Lapponica*, and the like, are strictly and exclusively alpine, *Arenaria Grœnlandica* and *Geum radiatum* (*Peckii*) are included for reasons which any botanist who has ascended these mountains will appreciate, although a form of the *Arenaria* sparingly occurs at low levels in Southern New England and New York, and both on the tops of the higher Alleghanies, where no characteristically alpine species accompany them, and where such summits as are bare of trees are not woodless on account of cold or any other incident of mere elevation.

Notwithstanding the geographical extent of the country over which it is spread, the North American alpine flora is meagre in species compared with that of Europe. This will abundantly appear in the comparison to be made in another part of this report. Reasons connected with geographical configuration and climate will account for this, but it must also be remembered that the botany of the European Alps is thoroughly known: that of the Rocky and other western mountains quite imperfectly so.

## II.—THE FOREST REGION.

### 1. *Its trees.*

The most conspicuous portion of the vegetation of a country, and the most important under more than one point of view, is its trees. Their importance is most manifest in the district under consideration, where less than a quarter of the area is capable of producing them, and of which, owing to fires and other causes, only about half of what Major Powell designates as "timber regions" are actually covered with forest. Toward the north the case is more or less altered, especially in British America, where, in a wide tract with moderately abundant and well distributed rainfall, and summers not excessively warm, the Atlantic and Pacific forests join and intermingle. Southward, and indeed nearly up to the northern boundary of the United States, trees are borne only on the mountains and high plateaux, and along the immediate banks of streams descending from these.

The species of the whole Rocky Mountain region (taken in the widest extent) which may claim the name of trees—even of tree-like shrubs—are not long to enumerate.* They are these:

| | |
|---|---|
| *Sapindus marginatus*, Willd. | *Morus microphylla*, Buckley. |
| *Acer grandidentatum*, Nutt. | *Populus angustifolia*, James. |
| *Negundo aceroides*, Moench. | *Populus balsamifera*, L. |

* We are much aided in this account by Prof. C. S. Sargent's article on The Forests of Central Nevada, in Amer. Journ. Sci., ser. 3, xvii, June, 1879, and by his Catalogue of the Forest Trees of North America, 1880, printed by the United States Census Bureau.

*Olneya Tesota*, Gray.
*Parkinsonia Torreyana*, Watson.
*Prosopis juliflora*, DC.
*Prosopis pubescens*, Benth.
*Acacia Greggii*, Gray.
*Prunus Pennsylvanica*, L.
*Cercocarpus ledifolius*, Nutt.
*Pyrus sambucifolia*, Cham. & Schl.
*Cratægus—near rivularis*, Nutt.
*Amelanchier alnifolia*, Nutt.
*Cereus giganteus*, Engelm.
*Sambucus glauca*, Nutt.
*Arbutus Menziesii*, Pursh, var.
*Fraxinus anomala*, Torr.
*Fraxinus pistaciæfolia*, Torr.
*Fraxinus viridis*, Michx., f.
*Chilopsis saligna*, Don.
*Platanus Wrightii*, Watson.
*Juglans Californica*, Watson.
*Juglans rupestris*. Engelm.
*Quercus Emoryi*, Torr.
*Quercus hypoleuca*, Engelm.
*Quercus undulata*, Torr.
*Betula occidentalis*, Hook.

*Populus Fremontii*, Watson.
*Populus monilifera*, Ait.
*Populus tremuloides*, Michx.
*Populus trichocarpa*, Torr. & Gray.
*Juniperus occidentalis*, Hook.
*Juniperus Californica*, Carr.
*Juniperus Virginiana*, L.
*Juniperus pachyphlœa*, Torr.
*Abies concolor*, Lindl.
*Abies subalpina*, Engelm.
*Pseudotsuga Douglasii*, Carr.
*Picea Engelmanni*, Engelm.
*Picea pungens*, Engelm.
*Larix occidentalis*, Nutt.
*Pinus edulis*, Engelm.
*Pinus flexilis*, James.
*Pinus aristata*, Engelm.
*Pinus Chihuahuana*, Engelm.
*Pinus contorta*, var. *Murrayana*, Eng.
*Pinus monophylla*, Torr.
*Pinus ponderosa*, Dougl., var. *scopulorum*, Engelm.
*Pinus Arizonica*, Engelm.
*Yucca brevifolia*, Engelm.

This mere botanical enumeration of about fifty species of trees, or at least arborescent plants, gives no proper idea of the arboreal flora as it presents itself to the view of a botanical traveler. It includes all the trees we know to inhabit any part of a vast tract, extending from the eastern base of the Rocky Mountains to the eastern base of the Sierra Nevada and Cascade ranges, and from the Mexican boundary, in latitude 32°, to the northern limit of forest, in about latitude 56°. The characters of the flora at the two extremes are most widely different. There is a far greater development of forest in the northern part, but it consists of the fewest species; and to the southern portion an undue appearance of richness is given to a very scanty sylva—first, by the enumeration of so many species which are only *arbusculæ* in their best estate, and are commonly mere shrubs; second, by including species, which belong only or mainly to the Mexican frontier region—to the southern part of Arizona and New Mexico.

Of the latter sort are *Yucca brevifolia*, the only monocotyledonous arborescent species (tree it cannot well be called); the giant Cactus, *Cereus giganteus*, of the Lower Gila district; *Pinus Chihuahuana* and *P. Arizonica*, which barely cross the Mexican line; *Sapindus marginatus*, *Arbutus Menziesii*, or what seems to be a mere geographical variety of the Californian Madroña, which is not uncommon in Mexico, and which reaches Southwestern Texas; *Fraxinus anomala* and *F. pistaciæfolia*,

*Platanus Wrightii*, &c., *Quercus Emoryi* and *Q. hypoleuca*, &c. Along with these, as equally foreign to the timber region of the Rocky Mountains and the accessory ranges, we should eliminate and place by themselves those trees which are characteristic of the southern arid plains, rather than of the mountains. A few of these come into Utah and Nevada, but they mostly belong to Arizona, and to a district, which, with all its aridity, receives a portion of the subtropical summer rainfall. To this category belong—

*Olneya Tesota*, a peculiar genus of papilionaceous *Leguminosæ*.

*Parkinsonia Torreyana*, the Palo Verde (*Cercidium* of authors).

*Prosopis juliflora*, the true Mesquite, and *P. pubescens*, the Screw Bean or Screw-pod Mesquite, the pods and seeds of which furnish food and forage, the bark a kind of gum-arabic, and the wood good fuel.

*Acacia Greggii*, the only one which in this district becomes aborescent.

*Chilopsis saligna*, the Desert Willow, fringing water-courses in the arid district.

*Morus microphylla*, a Texas Mulberry which extends along the southern part of New Mexico and Arizona.

It might be expected that a fair number of trees represented in the moister and cooler district of the Northern Rocky Mountains would disappear from the scantier, interrupted or scattered or restricted woods of the southern mountains; but we miss from them only one of the northern trees above enumerated, namely, the Larch of the region, *Larix occidentalis*, while we miss from the northern mountains no small number of those in the southern.

This is not the place to institute a comparison between the Rocky Mountain forest and the eastern; but it may be remarked that, while angiospermous, round-headed, and deciduous-leaved trees prevail in the latter, largely in the number of species and genera and conspicuously in the extent of surface occupied, the Rocky Mountain sylva, in its characteristic features, is gymnospermous, spiry, and evergreen. In the importance of its useful products, such as lumber, the difference between the two sorts, as a whole, in the Atlantic forest cannot be great. But with perhaps only one exception, that of the so-called Mountain Mahogany, *Cercocarpus ledifolius* (a small tree or more commonly a shrub), the economical value of the Rocky Mountain forest is almost wholly in its coniferous trees, and in the mountains these alone strike the eye.

Disregarding unessential and inconspicuous features, and eliminating those outlying small trees of the Mexican border, we may say that the Rocky Mountain forest is composed of the following species, which are arranged somewhat in the order of their conspicuousness and importance:

*Pinus ponderosa*, called Yellow Pine, and sometimes Long-leaved Pine, which distinguishes it well from the next. It is a composite species, and the form of it which we are concerned with, and to which Engelmann

assigns the name of *scopulorum* (*i. e.*, the Rocky Mountain variety), is
the one to which the term "long-leaved" least applies. It is one of the
largest trees of the proper Rocky Mountains, along which it ranges from
latitude 51°, according to Dr. G. M. Dawson, to, New Mexico, is rare on
any of the ranges which traverse the Nevada desert, and takes its fullest
development and predominance in California and Oregon, extending also
into the central dry region of British Columbia. It becomes a large
tree even on the interior mountains, in the southern part mostly on slopes
between 7,000 and 9,000 feet above the level of the sea, in the most
northern ceasing at three to four thousand. Its heavy and coarse-
grained lumber is suitable for the ruder building and the mining purposes to which it is devoted.

*Pinus contorta*, singularly called *Tamarack* in California, but in British
Columbia Bull or Black Pine, and in Utah Red Pine, is also a rather
composite species, one of equally great geographical range, but in higher
altitudes and latitude than the preceding. It replaces it on the mountains of Colorado at between eight or nine and ten or eleven thousand
feet ; is naturally absent from the Nevada and most of the Utah ranges ;
in British Columbia, according to young Dr. Dawson, " it is the characteristic tree over the northern part of the interior plateau, and densely
covers great areas. In the southern part of the province it is found only
on those parts of the plateau which rise above about 3,500 feet, where
the rainfall becomes too. great for the healthy growth of *P. ponderosa*.
It grows also abundantly on sandy beaches and river flats at less elevations." Loving moisture and coolness, it is also a coast species even
as far south as Mendocino County, California, whence it extends to the
Yukon River, in latitude 63°. Northeastward it gets beyond the Rocky
Mountains, in latitude 56°, and is replaced by the Banksian Pine " at
the watershed between the Athabasca and Saskatchewan." The wood
is white and light (so that the tree is sometimes called Spruce or White
Pine), but fairly durable ; but the tree never attains a great girth. In
Loudon's Encyclopædia of Trees and Shrubs, where this species is first
published on Douglas's specimens, it is named in English " The Twisted-
branched Pine." Douglas is thought to have given the name in reference to the dead and denudated slender lower branches, which persist
for a long while and curve downward and inward, but do not twist ; at
least this is the habit of the tree in the mountains. The trunk is per-
fectly straight.

*Pinus aristata* of Engelmann, the only form in our region of the earlier-
named *P. Balfouriana* of California (from which it differs only in the
armed tip of the cone-scales), is well called Fox-tail Pine from the appearance of the leafy branches, on which the closely set leaves persist
for a dozen years. It belongs only to high mountains and to latitudes
north of the forty-first parallel, and is nowhere found out of the drier
districts and their immediate borders. It is a small tree, of only botanical interest except in the mountains of Nevada, in the southern part of

which it abounds at the elevation of 7,500 or 8,000 feet, or rather once abounded, for, as Professor Sargent states, the trees within reach are fast being cut away to supply the mines with timbering. For this purpose its strong and close-grained, tough, and reddish wood is preferred to that of any other available tree.

*Pinus monophylla*, the single-leaved Nut Pine, is a most characteristic tree of the interior basin, mainly of the western and southern part of it, which it only slightly overpasses in Arizona and Southeastern California. It is a tree of slow growth, and of only ten to twenty feet in height, yet with trunk sometimes two feet in diameter, and with white and soft resinous wood, furnishing valuable fuel, and in this region of narrow choice it is much used for making charcoal. The great importance of the tree was, and still is, in the crop of large and delicately flavored seeds which it yields, constituting a staple article of food for the Indians of the Great Basin.

*Pinus edulis*, the Piñon or Nut Pine of the Southeastern Rocky Mountains, extends from the Arkansas to New Mexico and Arizona, a tree not larger than the foregoing, also has its importance in its edible seeds, and in the value of its wood for fuel.

*Pinus flexilis*, the White Pine of the Rocky Mountains, and belonging to the same general section as the Atlantic White Pine, but peculiar in its thick cones and good-sized edible seed, inhabits the higher region of the Rocky Mountains from Montana to New Mexico and the higher Nevada ranges. What is considered as a short-coned variety of it (*albicaulis*) is the highest tree, commonly reduced to a shrub, on and around alpine summits of the Sierra Nevada throughout all its length, and even northward in the Cascade Ranges to latitude 53°, in British Columbia. In the Rocky Mountain region this tree becomes large enough to be sawn into boards; and its light and soft wood is the best substitute for the Eastern white-pine lumber.

*Pseudotsuga Douglasii*, the Douglas Spruce, the most valuable timber tree of the west coast (with the possible exception of the Redwood), is hardly one of the second rank in such of the interior districts as it inhabits. But it is apparently absent from all the ranges west of the Uintas and south of the forty-second parallel until the western slope of the Sierra Nevada is reached, and is not very abundant in those of Colorado and New Mexico. It extends along the northern Rocky Mountains almost to latitude 54°, and a stunted variety descends on its eastern flanks. It is found scattered among other Coniferæ at middle elevations. But from Oregon to British Columbia, toward the coast and in the river valleys, this noble tree forms entire and vast forests, and takes a development in size and in numbers which is truly extraordinary. A large-fruited variety (*macrocarpa*) occurs at the southern extremity of the Sierra Nevada at no great elevation, and extends even into Mexico.

*Picea Engelmanni* (*Abies Engelmanni* of Parry, the discoverer), the

Spruce of the higher Rocky Mountains, is an important and good-sized timber-tree. It forms the principal part of the forest in Colorado between 8,500 and 11,000 feet, and at the upper tree-line is dwarfed to a shrub, accompanying *Pinus contorta*, but growing also at higher elevations. It is the representative of the Atlantic Spruces, in aspect and in the character of the lumber resembling Black Spruce, while the cones are just intermediate between those of the White Spruce and of the following. Distinct as they are on the whole in character and in station, it does seem as if these ran together in a series of specimens; while, on the other hand, on its northeastern limits, between the Peace River plateau and the Athabasca, east of the Rocky Mountains, in latitude 54° and 55°, *P. Engelmanni* seems to pass into *P. alba*. This species extends southward into Arizona, westward somewhat into the higher mountains of Nevada, and northwestward into the interior plateau of British Columbia. It should there be studied in its relations to *P. Sitchensis* of the northwest coast, the original *Abies Menziesii*.

*Picea pungens*, as Dr. Engelmann now calls it, the "*Abies Menziesii*" of Colorado, to the Rocky Mountains of which it is nearly confined, belongs to an elevational range just beneath that of *P. Engelmanni*, being sparsely associated with *Pinus ponderosa*, while the latter attends (and generally dominates) *P. contorta*, both, however, affecting moister soil, as is the habit of the Spruces. The timber of the two is probably not unlike. The rigid and prickly-pointed leaves render the name of *P. pungens* appropriate. This species takes kindly to cultivation both in England and in the Northern Atlantic States. A portion of the young trees display a very glaucous foliage, and are much admired.

*Abies concolor*, the more southern of the two Firs of the Rocky Mountains, accompanies *Picea Engelmanni* and *Pinus contorta* in the southern part of Colorado, and extends to New Mexico, where Fendler collected the specimens originally named. It passes westward in the mountains of Southern Utah and Arizona, and thence extends, according to Engelmann's identification, into and through the whole length of the Sierra Nevada, from 8,000 down to 3,000 or 4,000 feet of elevation, there becoming a pretty large tree. Its soft wood, like that of the eastern Balsam Firs, is of little account. The same is to be said of—

*Abies subalpina*, the more southern Rocky Mountain Fir, with smaller cones, which most resembles the eastern *A. balsamea*. This, from Central Colorado and from towards the upper forest limit, extends northward to British Columbia, and northeastward to beyond the mountains (where it may meet and even pass into the Balsam Fir), and northwestward perhaps almost to the Pacific coast. In the United States at least, it nowhere constitutes any important portion of the forest.

*Larix occidentalis*, the Western Larch, belongs only to the northern part of the Rocky Mountain forest region, and to the moister portion of this. Even there it seems to be an unimportant tree.

*Juniperus Virginiana*, the Red Cedar and Savin, is a tree of great range, as it extends from the Gulf of Saint Lawrence to that of Mexico, and northwestward into British Columbia, while southwestward it reaches Utah. In the Northern Rocky Mountains it is associated with *J. sabina*: in the Southern with the following species. Invaluable as its wood is, the tree is not large or abundant enough in the region under consideration to be of much account.

*Juniperus occidentalis* and *J. Californica*, the Western Red Cedars, have also a great range, a dubious variety of the former (too near a Mexican species) being the Cedar of Western Texas. The two in their various forms are very striking and characteristic trees of the dry interior region. Like the eastern species, they are sometimes mere shrubs, sometimes large but low trees.

*Juniperus pachyphlœa*, named for its very thick bark, which is likened to that of a Pine or of White Oak, takes the place of these species in Western New Mexico and adjacent parts of Arizona.

These are the trees of which the forest is composed, and which are the sole reliance for construction and fuel. Of their value to the country, of the importance to the country of their preservation, of the sad inroads that are made upon them by fires, and of their rapid consumption by the inhabitants, especially in mining, it is superfluous here to discourse.

The few angiospermous trees are of quite inferior importance, and the following are the only considerable ones:

*Cercocarpus ledifolius*, called Mountain Mahogany, is peculiar to the mountains of the Great Basin and of its borders. It is commonly a mere shrub, but at between 6,000 and 8,000 feet on the mountain sides it forms a small tree of 20 to 40 feet in height and a trunk which has in some cases reached the girth of 7 feet at base. The wood "is of a bright mahogany color, and susceptible of a beautiful polish, is exceedingly hard, heavy, and close grained, but very brittle, and so liable to heart-shake and difficult to work as to be useless in the arts. It is, however, sometimes employed for the bearings of machinery, where it is found to wear as well as metal." "It is," continues Professor Sargent, from whom these extracts are taken, "probably the only North American wood which is heavier than water," its specific gravity being determined by him to be 1.117 and its rate of growth so slow that "an examination of several specimens from one to two hundred years old shows an annual increase of wood only one-sixtieth of an inch in thickness."

*Negundo aceroides*, the Ash-leaved Maple, is found in valleys along water-courses in the southern part of the Rocky Mountains, and as far west as the Wahsatch, and south to New Mexico and Arizona, while in California it is represented by a closely allied species. Its eastern extension is to Canada and the borders of New England. Sugar is sometimes made from its sap.

More important and conspicuous are the Poplars, which, growing wherever there is running water traversing even very arid districts, form a feature where streams issue from the mountains, and are the principal available shade-trees in places artificially irrigated, while their soft white wood is of some account in the absence of better. The Poplars of this kind, or the Cottonwoods of the region, are:

*Populus monilifera*, the Eastern Cottonwood, which reaches the eastern slope of the Rocky Mountains, but probably does not cross them.

*Populus Fremonti*, a Californian species, a doubtful variety of which (or perhaps *P. Mexicana*) is the prevalent Cottonwood of the southern part of the interior district.

*Populus trichocarpa*, a kind of Balsam Poplar, which ranges from British Columbia to Southern California, and reaches Western Nevada.

*Populus balsamifera* and its broad-leaved variety, *candicans*, Northeastern Poplars, which reach and more or less cross the Rocky Mountains; and the related—

*Populus angustifolia*, the common Balsam Poplar of the middle part of the whole region under consideration.

*Populus tremuloides*, the American Aspen, is perhaps the most widely distributed of North American trees, and economically one of the most insignificant, except that the soft wood is used of late for paper pulp, and in Utah it is said to be employed in turnery and for flooring. It ranges from the Arctic coast to all the cooler parts of the Atlantic States, through the Rocky Mountains to New Mexico and Arizona, and on the western side of the continent to the middle of California. It is always a small tree, fond of moist bottoms and slopes, but on the higher mountains southward it takes to the higher ridges, and forms thick copses toward the upper limit of tree growth.

*Betula occidentalis* is a sparing but somewhat noteworthy element of the Rocky Mountain forest along its northern border in British Columbia, and is found down to Colorado and New Mexico, yet only as a shrub; also along the Sierra Nevada, where, at its southern known limit, above Owen's Valley, and in a dry region bordering the Great Basin, "it is reported to be abundant, and often the main reliance of the settlers for timber for fencing and other purposes." (Bot. Calif., ii, 79.)

From the whole region Oaks are conspicuously absent as trees, though *Quercus undulata* and the forms referred to it are prominent as shrubs southward on the eastern slopes of the Colorado Rocky Mountains, and around them into New Mexico and Arizona, and although one or two Mexican types, such as *Q. hypoleuca*, *Q. Emoryi*, and *Q. reticulata*, form small trees in the southern portions of Arizona.

The shrubby vegetation might be taken into account in connection with the forest growth. But in this region, where almost everything that is perennial becomes more or less lignescent, and where a predominant part of the vegetation of the woodless districts is suffruticose, the herbs and shrubs may as well go together.

Without entering here into a comparison of the Rocky Mountain forest with any other, it may be noted that the species are peculiar to the region or the vicinity of it, with a few exceptions. *Prunus Pennsylvanica, Populus balsamifera, monilifera,* and *tremuloides,* may be said to come in from the northeast, and only the last extends far into the district. The *Negundo* and *Juniperus Virginiana,* with *Fraxinus viridis,* belong to the Atlantic forest region, and do not penetrate far, unless we count the Californian *Negundo* as a derivative form. The connection with Pacific forest species is closer; and for the rest they are mainly Mexican plateau types, of which the botanical district in question may be regarded as a northern extension.

2. *Characteristics of the herbaceous and shrubby vegetation of the Rocky Mountain forest region.*

It was convenient and, indeed, needful to take the sylva of this region into one view, extending from British Columbia to New Mexico and Arizona, and from the Rocky Mountains to the western verge of the Great Basin. But in its northern part the distinction between woodland and woodless country is less marked, and the general botany is comparatively homogeneous throughout the whole latitude, the Atlantic and Pacific forests being there in fact confluent. Along the southern border, under very different conditions and with little and sparse forest, there is an analogous intermingling of the botanical elements, and the general vegetation of these wide-apart extremes is very different. Our personal observations were made on a middle and typical belt, on which the botany of the central region under notice is most largely developed and purely exhibited, and where Atlantic and Pacific botany are most widely separated geographically. We shall do well, therefore, to restrict our sketches to this central belt, comprising Colorado and the southern part of Wyoming on the east, Utah in the center, and Nevada at the west.

And when treating of the vegetation which is fostered by the forest, there is, in fact, only the eastern half of the district to consider, i. e., the proper Rocky Mountains, the Wahsatch, and the Uintas, which connect these two systems. Far westward, throughout the Great Basin proper, there is not forest enough to impress any botanical character upon the humbler growth, although wherever there is moisture there is a vegetation to correspond.

As has already been suggested, the timber region is more extensive than the grounds actually bearing forest. The contraction of the latter to its present limits is, no doubt, largely a consequence of forest fires through a long course of years; but we suppose that it is also due to an antecedent or accompanying stage of increasing desiccation of the country—a stage which, however, had passed its crisis before our acquaintance with the region began, the turn being testified to by the increase in the height of the water in the Great Salt Lake during the last thirty or forty years. We shall not strain the facts, in any case, if we include in the botany of the forest region, not only the plants which are now sheltered by forest, but those which extend either downward or

2 G B

upward over ground which might well nourish the same kind of tree growth. This is the vegetation of the mountains, as distinguished from that of the high plains.

The peculiar shrubs of the Rocky Mountains (including the Wahsatch Range and corresponding ranges farther north) are only *Jamesia Americana*, a Hydrangeous genus of no near affinity to any other, except *Fendlera*, which (equally unique) belongs to a lower region in New Mexico and Western Texas, *Robinia Neo-Mexicana*, which is an outlying species on the southeastern border, *Quercus undulata*, *Rubus deliciosus*, *Philadelphus microphyllus*, *Ceanothus Fendleri*, and *Berberis Fendleri*, the latter a species of the *Vulgaris* type. They are all southern; the Northern Rocky Mountains have no characteristic shrub, as they have no characteristic tree. The principal shrubs which they share with the Pacific forest region are *Acer glabrum*, *Prunus demissa*, *Rubus Nutkanus*, *Spiræa discolor*, *Ribes*, 3 or 4 species, *Symphoricarpus oreophilus* and *rotundifolius*, *Ledum glandulosum*, *Salix Geyeriana*, and, if we come down to such low frutescent growth, *Pachystima Myrsinites*, and *Berberis repens*.

*Arctostaphylos pungens*, a species of the Mexican plateau, which appears to have taken a wonderful development and diversification in California, of which it is the prevalent shrub, has reached the western portion of the Rocky Mountain Region as high in latitude as the forty-first parallel, and at an altitude which brings it among the forest shrubbery.

The shrubs which are common to this and to the Atlantic forests are not numerous nor of sufficient interest to be specified. They are such as *Ampelopsis*, *Cornus stolonifera*, and the like. The genus *Shepherdia*, however, is somewhat noteworthy. *S. argentea*, the Buffalo Berry, which seems most at home in the Northeastern Rocky Mountains, and which extends much beyond them in the same direction, along with its relative *Elæagnus argentea*, extends southward even to New Mexico, and westward to the Sierra forming that rim of the Great Basin; and it is accompanied by *S. Canadensis*, a characteristic shrub of the northern border of the Atlantic forest. The third species of the genus is peculiar to Southern Nevada.

Of the shrubs which traverse the continent and completely enter the Pacific forest the following are the principal:

| | |
|---|---|
| *Rhus glabra*. | *Betula glandulosa*. |
| *Rhus aromatica*. | *Alnus incana ?* |
| *Neillia opulifolia*. | *Corylus rostrata*. |
| *Pyrus sambucifolia*. | *Juniperus communis*. |
| *Symphoricarpus racemosus*. | *Juniperus sabina ?* |
| *Symphoricarpus occidentalis*. | *Arctostaphylos Ura-Ursi*, if we con- |
| *Lonicera involucrata*. | descend to one so low. |
| *Sambucus racemosus* (*pubens*). | |

The last three and the *Sambucus* are of the Old World, North Asiatic as well as European. They are all of northern range, and are there somewhat continuous across the continent, although extending well southward along the mountains.

A full analysis of the herbaceous vegetation would run too far into details. We can mention only the peculiar types and some of the genera which are characteristically prominent.

The three genera (each of a single species) which are wholly restricted to the Rocky Mountains are *Chionophila*, which is strictly alpine, and has been already mentioned as such, and *Leucampyx*, an Anthemideous Composita (both of southern habitat), and *Orogenia*, S. Watson, a little Umbelliferous plant, with habit of *Erigenia*, but too little known to speak of.

*Synthyris*, a Scrophulariaceous genus of seven species, is a characteristic but not quite a peculiar type, one of the seven species being of more western habitat, and one on the eastern verge of the Atlantic region.

*Hesperochiron* of S. Watson is a peculiar Hydrophyllaceous type, but both species occur also in the Sierra Nevada.

*Lewisia* is a most characteristic and almost peculiar genus; but the original species has been found even in California, and a second one occurs on the southwestern rim of the Great Basin.

*Townsendia* is a highly characteristic genus, but some species belong to the alpine regions above and some to the dry plains below the forest region, and a few have a more western range.

*Sidalcea candida* is a restricted species of a genus peculiar to our and a more western region.

*Glycosma, Cynapium* of Nuttall (now in *Ligusticum*), *Camassia, Corydalis Caseana, Parnassia fimbriata, Gaultheria Myrsinites*, and the considerable genera *Wyethia* and *Helianthella*, are in very similar case.

*Calochortus* is a most characteristic type of numerous species, some of the Rocky Mountains, more of them Californian, and a few Mexican.

*Adenocaulon bicolor* (of a peculiar genus, which is also both Eastern Asiatic and Chilian) is rather a western coast plant, which has traversed the Rocky Mountains at the north, even to Lake Superior.

*Frasera*, a marked and wholly North American genus, has given one species to the Atlantic forest, and shared two or three with the western region.

But the characteristic features of the Rocky Mountain herbaceous vegetation in the region specified, taken as a whole and in reference to abundance both of forms and of individuals, are imparted by the following genera, which have assumed their maximum development in and west of these mountains, and are mainly if not quite peculiar to North America.

*Gilia, Collomia, Phlox,* and *Polemonium*, of the order *Polemoniaceæ.*

*Pentstemon, Castilleia,* and *Mimulus*, of the order *Scrophulariaceæ;* and *Pedicularis* here takes its principal American development in the higher regions.

*Phacelia* in *Hydrophyllaceæ*, but most of the species are below the forest district and of westward range.

*Eriogonum* of *Polygonaceæ*, of which the same is to be said, although a few species are conspicuous in the wooded region.

*Compositæ* are very prominent, as they are throughout North America, and the genus *Aplopappus* might be added to the foregoing; but the most characteristic genera are not in the wooded region. There, too, the species of *Solidago* and of *Aster* are less numerous than at the East, and *Erigeron* is more prominent than *Aster*.

The number of species of *Astragalus* in the Rocky Mountain and more western districts is inferior only to those of Asia, but they mostly affect the unwooded plains.

Peculiar to and conspicuous in the cooler wooded region are the two beautiful long-spurred species of *Aquilegia*, *A. cærulea* and *A. chrysantha*, the former alpestrine, the latter at lower elevations, neither found north of Colorado.

A few of the Rocky Mountain wooded-region shrubs occur on the higher mountains and ravines of the Great Basin, probably more of them than are yet recorded. Of additional species only two come to mind, and both are peculiar. They are—

*Shepherdia rotundifolia* of Parry, in the mountains of Southern Utah.

*Peraphyllum ramosissimum*, Nutt., a peculiar Pomaceous genus, along the western rim of the Great Basin.

A few other higher-mountain species of *Ceanothus* come in from California, as to various herbs; but we call to mind no characteristic species of the basin which belong unequivocally to the forest district.

### III.—WOODLESS REGIONS BELOW FOREST.

These may be distinguished into the lower mountain slopes, the western arid district, of which the so-called Great Basin is the center and the exemplar, and the less arid, unbroken plains east of the proper Rocky Mountains.

1. *The Lower Rocky Mountain Slopes*, including the "parks," so called, of Colorado and valleys which are not condemned to a saline vegetation, partake of the growth above and below, but they have a good number of characteristic plants. The prevalent characteristic shrubs are largely Rosaceous. They are:

*Cercocarpus parvifolius*, along with *C. ledifolius* when that is not reckoned among the trees; the former a species which is even more common on all Californian foot-hills. These districts are the headquarters of this peculiar genus, although the latter was founded on a Mexican species.

*Cowania Mexicana*, which is likewise Mexican, as the name intimates.

*Purshia tridentata*, which extends much farther north than the others, but not ascending above the base of the mountains.

*Spiræa discolor*, which in its various forms flourishes under exceedingly different altitudes.

*Spiræa Millefolium*, which is quite peculiar to the Great Basin.

*Spiræa cæspitosa* should be added, although it spreads in mats over the face of rocks, concealing its trunk, instead of rising into the air.

*Coleogyne ramosissima*, a highly peculiar genus of a single species, found only on the southern border of the Great Basin.

*Prunus Andersonii*, of the Amygdaleous type, restricted to its southwestern rim.

Hardly elsewhere is such an assemblage to be found. Of other shrubs, *Ceanothus velutinus* and *Ribes cereum* are the most widespread and abundant. One species of *Ephedra* extends along the mountains almost to the northern border of the Great Basin, and two or three more are among the characteristic shrubs of the region south of it.

As to herbs, the genera and the groups mentioned above as predominant at a greater elevation (especially *Gilia*, *Pentstemon*, *Phacelia*, and *Eriogonum*) still play a prominent part. *Astragali* become more numerous, as also do white-flowered species of *Œnothera*, and Helianthoideous, Helenioideous, and Senecionoideous Compositæ are conspicuous, yet not more so than in other parts of North America. Few Compositæ are peculiar to this zone, and few genera are peculiar to the Rocky Mountain region as distinguished from the Californian. The more characteristic genera of the whole region may be adverted to in another connection.

2. *The arid or desert interior district*, namely, that between the Rocky Mountains and the Sierra Nevada, the central part of which is the Great Basin proper, with no exterior drainage, but which also extends far north between the Rocky Mountains and the Cascades, and is there drained by the Columbia River, and far south over the district through which flow the waters of Rio Colorado and the Gila, with also an extensive eastern outlier between the Wahsatch and the Colorado Rocky Mountains, and, as well, north of the Uintas, drained by the Green River, the main and farthest source of the Colorado, where an arid woodless tract, with all the features of the Great Basin, broadly intersects the wooded Rocky Mountain ranges. The mountains which traverse and diversify these deserts are thought to occupy about half the area, and although many of them appear to be as bare as the intervening valleys, yet their varied surface and exposure and the condensation of moisture which they compel, even from an unwilling air, nourish a different vegetation, consisting of a larger number of species. This having already been noted, only the botany of the valleys and plains is under present consideration.

The region, in a general botanical view, is one of *undershrubbiness;* and the prevalent growth is composed of *Artemisias*, *Chenopods*, and lignescent small-flowered Compositæ. It cannot be better described than in the terms employed by Mr. Watson in King's Exploration (Rep. **xxiv, xxv**), which is here accordingly cited:

"No portion of this whole district, however desert in repute and in fact, is destitute of some amount of vegetation even in the driest seasons, excepting only the alkali flats, which are usually of quite limited extent. Even these have frequently a scattered growth of *Sarcobatus* or *Halostachys*, surmounting isolated hillocks of drifted sand, compacted by their roots and buried branches.

"This vegetation, covering alike the valley plains, the graded incline of the mesas, the rounded foot-hills, and the mountain slopes, possesses a monotonous sameness of aspect, and is characterized mainly by the absence of trees, by the want of a grassy-green sward, the wide distribution of a few low shrubs or half-shrubby plants, to the apparent exclusion of nearly all other growth, and by the universally prevalent gray or dull olive color of the herbage. * * * The turfing 'Buffalo' or 'Grama' Grasses, which make the plains east of the Rocky Mountains a vast pasture for the bison, deer, and antelope, are here unknown. There are, indeed, various other species more or less abundant in localities, but always growing in sparsely scattered turfs and dying away with the early summer heats, or to be then found only in favored spots in the mountain cañons. Two or three species that may be said to mat into a sward are confined to alkaline meadows, and are nearly worthless for pasturage.

"Of the more predominant species which form the mass of the shrubby and perennial vegetation of the entire region, some are confined almost wholly to the more saline localities. Of these the *Halostachys occidentalis* is an exclusively alkaline shrub, growing where almost no other plant will. Much more widely distributed and abundant is the *Sarcobatus vermiculatus*, found nearly everywhere in the lower valleys where there is a decided amount of alkali, but rarely extending much beyond such limits. The more frequent plants accompanying these are *Salicornia herbacea* and several species of *Suæda*, and other mostly Chenopodiaceous plants, and, if there are grasses at all, *Brizopyrum spicatum* and *Spartina gracilis*.

"On the somewhat less alkaline and drier portion of the valleys are found in frequent abundance *Atriplex confertifolia* and *canescens*, or the nearly as common *Grayia polygaloides*, and rather less abundantly *Artemisia spinescens*, *Eurotia lanata*, and *Kochia prostrata*. Sometimes mingled with them, but wholly free from alkaline preferences, and beyond their range usurping entire predominance, is the 'Everlasting Sage Brush,' the *Artemisia tridentata*. This is by far the most prevalent of all species, covering valleys and foot-hills in broad stretches further than the eye can reach, the growth never so dense as to seriously obstruct the way, but very uniform over large surfaces, very rarely reaching the saddle-height of a mule, and ordinarily but half that altitude.

"The 'Broom Sage' *Bigelovia graveolens* occurs in considerable abundance along the dry valleys, often accompanied by *Tetradymia canescens ;* but upon the gravelly foot-hills the smaller *Bigelovia Douglasii* is much more frequent."

One or two names are changed in copying so as to conform to the more recent nomenclature. *Eurotia lanata,* though it happens not to come into the above extract, is among the commonest of these plants, and is one of the widest in range. Some *Astragali,* various *Eriogona* and *Gilia,* also several *Phacelia* and *Œnothera,* would be next in prominence, the *Eriogona* much the most so. But the peculiarity of the basin flora lies as much in the absence of other genera which characterize adjacent districts as in the ubiquity of those which have been mentioned.

The genera peculiar, or nearly so, to the Great Basin proper and its borders are chiefly—

*Physaria,* a genus which was confounded on mere habit with *Vesicaria,* belonging to the foot-hills rather than to the valleys, the principal species extending around the whole limits of the region, a peculiar one at the north and another at the south.

*Platyspermum,* Hook., a little Cruciferous annual of the western border.

*Purshia,* DC., a Rosaceous shrub, already mentioned.

*Tricardia* and *Conanthus,* of S. Watson, Hydrophyllaceous herbs, the latter close to *Nama,* the former a peculiar genus.

*Oryctes,* Watson, a rather obscure Solanaceous herb of Western Nevada.

*Nitrophila,* Watson, an Amarantaceous herb of alkaline soil.

*Grayia,* Hook., a Chenopodiaceous undershrub, already enumerated as one of the most characteristic of the desert plants. (*Sarcotatus* would go with it, except that it crosses the Rocky Mountains and abounds on the upper waters of the Missouri, where it was first known, being the Pu py Thorn of Lewis and Clark.)

*Hermidium,* Watson, a Nyctagineous perennial of the western edge of the basin, intermediate between *Bougainvillea* and *Mirabilis.*

*Oxytheca,* Nutt., an offshoot of the great genus *Eriogonum.*

*Tetradymia,* DC., characteristic shrubby Senecioneous Compositæ of two or three species, which slightly overpass the borders of the basin.

*Glyptopleura,* Eaton, of two species, and *Anisocoma,* Gray, of one, depressed Cichoraceous annuals or biennials.

*Chætadelpha, Blepharipappus,* and *Rigiopappus,* each of a single species, and *Psathyrotes* of two, southern in range, also Compositæ.

There is, besides, *Caulanthus* of S. Watson, of two or three very characteristic desert species, but some Californian, and the genus is only artificially distinguished from *Streptanthus,* species of which reach the Pacific coast on the one hand and Missouri to Texas on the other.

*Eremochloe,* S. Watson, is a peculiar genus of grasses, one species peculiar to the basin, another to the southeastern part of New Mexico.

The arid region south of the Great Basin we propose only in a general way to refer to. It is one in which there is no barrier to the spreading of the same species from the Gulf of California to the Gulf of Mexico, and in which the plants of the basin region, of Southern California, of Texas, and of the Mexican plateau and mountains meet and mingle. This district has also a good number of peculiar genera of shrubs: *Salazaria*, in Labiatæ; *Holacantha*, a spiny Simarubacea; *Canotia*, a rather doubtful Rutacea, to which might be added *Thamnosma* except that a second species is Texan; and *Chilopsis*, which extends into Mexico; among herbs, *Canbya*, a singular little Papaveracea; *Petalonyx*, in Loasaceæ (also *Cevallia*, which extends both to Texas and Mexico); *Hesperocallis*, in Liliaceæ; *Dithyræa*, which has been joined to the Old World genus *Biscutella*; *Wislizena* and *Oxystylis*, in Capparidaceæ; *Achyronychia*, in Illecebraceæ; and among Compositæ the genera *Baileya*, *Riddellia*, *Hymenoclea*, *Hymenothrix;* and here also are the headquarters of *Laphamia* and *Perityle*.

### 3. *The eastern woodless plains.*

If the arid district of the interior of the United States west of the eastern Rocky Mountains is denominated the region of "Sage Brush" (*i. e.*, of shrubby *Artemisia* and *Chenopods*), the mostly less arid, less saline, equally homogeneous, and even more extensive plains between the Rocky Mountains and the eastern forest region may be characterized as the region of Buffalo Grasses. Its full development is between latitude 35° and 45°, where it occupies an average of ten degrees of longitude. North of this it is narrowed or interrupted, and then merges into a district which is woodless from cold or from the nature of the soil, and at length arctic. Southward it is equally broad, and it trends westward and loses itself in the New Mexican plateau region, which has a certain character of its own, but in which the eastern forms of vegetation mingle first with those of the Rocky Mountains, with those of the Mexican plateau, and at length with those which prevail in the Great Basin.

The whole region rises very gradually westward and abuts against the mountains at an elevation of, for the most part, fully 5,000 feet. The annual rainfall on its eastern border is from 24 to 32 inches, tolerably well distributed; in its western part 14 to 16 inches. Upon the climatic characteristics, topography, &c., which have been well presented in various reports and summaries, especially in those published by Dr. Hayden, it is not our purpose to enter.

Nor have we here any special call to discuss the vexed "prairie question," viz, why it is that the eastern border of this broad district should be treeless, except along river banks, even where the annual rainfall is from 28 to 32 inches, and 8 to 10 inches of this in summer—as much rain as is in the upper part of Michigan and on the Canada shore of Lake Huron; also why prairies exist as deep bays or islands within the Atlantic forest region. Suffice it to note that the prairies east of the Mississippi are mainly restricted to places having little or no more rainfall than that mentioned above; also that where annual fires have been prevented, original prairie surfaces are changing into forests,* and that, generally, trees properly planted or raised from seed, with some nursing at the start, are found to thrive along this whole border.

In view of this, and of the well-known habit of the Indians to burn over the dry vegetation of the plains and prairies in autumn, we had thought it most probable "that the line of demarkation between our woods and our plains is not where it was drawn by nature"; that "between the ground which receives rain enough for forest and that which receives too little, there must be a debatable border, where comparatively slight causes will turn the balance either way," and where "difference in soil and exposure will tell decisively." And along this border, annual burnings, for the purpose of increasing and improving buffalo feed, practiced for hundreds of years by our nomade predecessors, may have had a very marked effect in carrying this woodless district farther eastward than it otherwise might have reached.†

Along with this, a more hypothetical cause may be assigned, which, if valid, will help in other explanations. That natural rain-gauge, the Great Salt Lake in Utah, informs us that the rainfall is now increasing over the western border of the region under consideration. We know what the maximum height of the water was very long ago; but we know not the minimum. It is not improbable that this era of increasing moisture is of no recent commencement, but has supervened on an earlier one of greater dryness than the present, and that this affected the great plains east, as well as the great basin west, of the interposed Rocky Mountains. In that case districts may now bear forest, under man's care, which would have been incapable of it before this cycle commenced or had attained the present condition.

The western portion of these plains is not only drier, but in some parts alkaline, or with other characters of soil uncongenial to forage grasses, especially at the north, where there are only two inches of rain in the three summer and no more in the three winter months. A good deal of the southern part gets about four inches of summer rain, but only half as much in winter. In some parts, accordingly, the characteristic vegetation of the ultramontane plateau intrudes. The Pulpy Thorn, *Sarcobatus*, and its Chenopodeous associates are largely developed on the Upper Missouri waters, accompanied by a peculiar Sage-Brush, *Artemesia cana*, while the *A. tridentata* is rather rarely established on this side of the mountains.

We have termed this district the region of Buffalo Grass. The grasses form such an inconspicuous and unimportant a feature in the interior arid region that it has not been worth while to mention them, and even on the mountains, except in the alpine region, they are of small account.

---

* *Vide* Prof. C. A. White, in Amer. Jour. Sci., Oct., 1878.
† See Forest Geography and Archæology, in Amer. Jour. Sci., 1878, Ser. 3, XVI, 94,—

On the eastern plains they are the characteristic feature. When we get beyond the eastern prairie border, the grasses of which are prevailingly eastern in character, we come upon plains which are generally covered with the very low and tufted grasses peculiar to the drier plains, which form, if not a sward, yet something which serves as a substitute for it, not green, except in early spring, but of a dull grayish hue, and the characteristic species usually rising only a hand-breadth above the surface. These are the Buffalo Grasses or Bunch Grasses, which have nourished hordes of bison and flocks of antelopes down to a few years ago, and which are now the capital of the herdsmen or ranchmen, and the nutritious food of increasing numbers of domestic cattle.

The Buffalo Grass, *par excellence*, and by its abundance, is *Buchloë dactyloides* of Engelmann. This is a diœcious Chlorideous grass, the male and the comparatively scarce female plants of which were very naturally thought to be of quite different genera until their relationship was suspected and determined by Dr. Engelmann, and this apt name was applied to it.

*Munroa squarrosa* of Torrey (*Crypsis squarrosa*, Nutt.), another much depressed and peculiar Chlorideous grass, is next in importance. Both are wholly peculiar to this region.

*Bouteloua*, a Chlorideous genus of a more ordinary type, of several species, chiefly endemic to this region and to corresponding districts in Mexico, is the third in rank. These are the "*Grama*" Grasses—a name which probably came from the Spanish. They are taller, of sparser growth, and make good forage.

*Pleuraphis Jamesi*, Torr., is a Buffalo Grass peculiar to the southern part of the region, with some westward extension.

*Vaseya comata*, Gray, represents another peculiar genus; but the species extends to the Californian region.

*Eriocoma cuspidata* is the Bunch Grass of the very driest soils, and naturally extends across the Great Basin.

*Sporobolus airoides*, Torr., abounds over the whole length of the region and beyond it, in the more low and subsaline soils. It is accompanied by *Beckmannia* (also a North Asiatic grass), by *Distichlis maritima*, by one or two wide-spread species of *Atropis*, &c. The drier ground in many places bears species of *Stipa* and *Aristida*. *Hordeum jubatum* and the peculiar *Elymus Sitanion* are characteristic grasses.

Of other dominant and more or less peculiar forms of vegetation—having chiefly in view the central tract—we should mention a great white-flowered *Argemone* (*A. hispida*, Gray); *Stanleya*, and the greater part of the known species of *Vesicaria*; *Cleome integrifolia*; the whole genus *Callirrhoë*; a *Krameria*; a *Glycyrrhiza*; the herbaceous *Sophora sericea*; the principal development of the peculiar genus *Petalostemon*, and southward numerous species of *Dalea* (which go on increasing into Mexico): also of *Psoralea*; most of the species of *Gaura*, several of *Œnothera*, and the peculiar genus *Stenosiphon*, allied to *Gaura*; a good number of *Cac-*

*taceæ* (chiefly *Opuntia* and *Mamillariæ*), increasing southward; a thick-rooted perennial *Cucurbita* (*perennis*), with some relatives southwestward; the species of *Machæranthera*, or biennial Asters; *Aplopappus spinulosus* and some other species; *Bigelovia* and *Gutierrezia* in characteristic forms which are shared with the ultramontane arid district, and a great development of Senecionoid Compositæ, perhaps not exceeding the other parts of the United States, yet more conspicuous to the eye; the two species of *Solanum* with prickly calyx closed over the fruit; *Pentstemon* in species equaled only by California; *Hedeoma* and *Monarda*; *Leucocrinum*, which, however, extends westward.

Besides those variously mentioned, a goodly number of genera are peculiar to this and the more western districts, which we need not here enumerate. Of absolutely peculiar genera, there is *Selenia*, in Cruciferæ; *Cristatella*, in Capparidaceæ; *Musenium, Polytænia*, and *Trepocarpus*, in Umbelliferæ; *Thelesperma* (except for a Buenos Ayrean species), *Engelmannia, Bradburia, Diaperia*, &c., among Compositæ; *Stephanomeria, Lygodesma* and *Troximon* are very characteristic Cichoraceous genera, which also abound far westward.

The characteristics of the Rocky Mountain flora—whether taken as a broad whole or in its constituent geographical parts—are in no small degree negative. What this flora lacks is perhaps more remarkable than what it possesses. This will appear on a comparison of the vegetation of the three great regions: the Atlantic naturally wooded region; the Central region, woodless except on mountains; the Pacific region, largely but not wholly wooded.

## II.

### COMPARISON OF THE ATLANTIC, PACIFIC, AND ROCKY MOUNTAIN REGION FLORAS.

A full and critical comparison would require a tabulation of the genera and species of the North American flora, and of their geographical distribution, and this would be a large and difficult undertaking.

Even the sketch of the principal or salient features, which we may here present, it is best to confine to the central belt, along which the three regions are particularly well defined, namely, to the United States north of the peninsula of Florida (which has considerable tropical vegetation) and of Texas, leaving out of view the Texano-Arizonian region, which, with the adjacent parts of Mexico, has in general a vegetation of its own, and is not very distinctly separable into wooded and woodless, or even into eastern, middle, and western, districts. The same is the case, in a different way, in the country north of the United States boundary, as has been already explained.

The comparison attempted is, therefore, that of the flora of the Atlantic States between the Gulf of St. Lawrence and the Gulf of Mexico, on the one hand, with that of California and Oregon and with the broad district between them, stretching from the plains of Arkansas to Dakota on the east to the Sierra Nevada and Cascade Mountains on the west. Then the alpine vegetation, already treated of, is left out of view, except in the case of endemic genera or forms not belonging to to the arctic-alpine flora. And it must be kept in mind that the eastern slopes and outliers of the Sierra and its continuation, below the wooded portions, belong to the Great Basin or to the region reckoned with it. So we do not reckon *Pinus monophylla*, nor *Chilopsis saligna*, nor *Leucocrinum*, and the like, as common to the Great Basin and the Pacific floras, but as pertaining to the former only; and generally we do not take account of species which merely overpass the border of the region they belong to. For example, we should not reckon *Anemone Nuttalliana*, nor *Dalea alopecuroides*, nor *Collinsia parviflora*, and hardly *Rubus Nutkanus* as constituents of the Atlantic United States flora. Such limitations heighten the contrast between the compared floras, but render the comparison more manageable and effective, and also, as to the broad outlines, really more faithful to nature than they would be if the materials were indiscriminately collected from the descriptive books and every denizen of the frontiers regarded as a true citizen.

All naturalized plants and weeds of cultivation are, of course, neglected, including such as may be of American origin but which have accompanied man, even the aborigines of the country, almost everywhere. They belong to no particular flora, or at least are not characteristic of any.

The natural orders may be taken up *seriatim*.

RANUNCULACEÆ.—Are represented on the Atlantic side by eighteen genera, on the Pacific by fourteen, in the intermediate region (the Rocky Mountain flora in the broadest sense) by twelve. The species are in nearly the same relative proportion, and a considerable number are common even to all three floras, the most striking case of this being that of *Clematis (Atragene) verticillaris*. All the genera of the Rocky Mountain flora (if we except *Crossosoma*) are amphigæan.* Of such genera, *Pæonia* is peculiar to the Pacific, and *Hepatica* (if ranked as a genus) only to the Atlantic flora. The peculiar genera are *Trautvetteria*, Atlantic and Pacific; *Hydrastis* and *Xanthorrhiza*, wholly Alleghanian; and *Crossosoma* of California, a genus of dubious affinity, but probably nearest *Pæonia*, in two species, one which belongs to the Arizonian district. The species of *Delphinium* increase from the Atlantic westward, and are remarkably prominent in California.

MAGNOLIACEÆ.—Of three genera and eleven species in the Atlantic flora; are wholly absent from the westward floras.

ANONACEÆ.—Have a peculiar genus (the so-called Papaw) in the Atlantic flora, but nothing to the west of it.

* This is the most convenient designation of the genera indigenous to Europe and Northern Asia as well as to America.

MENISPERMACEÆ.—Of three genera and as many species in the Atlantic flora; are equally wanting westward.

BERBERIDACEÆ.—This is a marked family in North America. The amphigæan genus *Berberis* has genuine Atlantic and one (southern) Rocky Mountain species; the western mountains have a characteristic and common low *Mahonia* (and another on the southern border); and there are two or three more on the Pacific side. Of herbaceous types the whole central region has none; the Pacific coast has *Vancouveria* and *Achlys*, peculiar genera of single species; the Atlantic has those four special genera, *Caulophyllum, Diphylleia, Jeffersonia*, and *Podophyllum* peculiar to it and to Northeastern Asia, of single species to each continent.

NYMPHÆACEÆ.—Of the typical genera, *Nymphæa* is represented only in the Atlantic flora and by two peculiar species (with others in Florida and Texas), and *Nuphar* by three species; a peculiar *Nuphar* belongs to the two western floras. *Nelumbium* has only an Atlantic species, which even reaches to the West Indies. *Brasenia*, that genus and single species of wonderful distribution, is common on the eastern and not very rare on the western coast. *Cabomba* is peculiarly Atlantic.

SARRACENIACEÆ.—This wholly American order of Pitcher-plants has its leading genus of six species confined to the Atlantic border; a single curious representative, *Darlingtonia*, on the mountains of California; the third genus is on a mountain in Guiana.

PAPAVERACEÆ.—This small order, the typical genus of which is represented in America only by an arctic-alpine species, has its largest and most remarkable generic diversification in North America, and in the belt of country now under observation, partly on the Atlantic yet more strikingly on the Pacific side. But, except for an *Argemone* which is very conspicuous over the great plains, and the alpine *Papaver*, sparingly met with on the highest peaks, the order is absent from the Rocky Mountain flora in general. No European type is indigenous to Eastern North America, and only one of the American is Japano-Asiatic, viz. *Stylophorum*, of course on the Atlantic side. The other Atlantic genus is *Sanguinaria*, which has no fellow. But California has a species of the European genus *Meconopsis* and the following endemic genera: *Romneya* of Southern California, with a large poppy-like flower; *Arctomecon*, poppy-like, except in its stigmas and the anomaly of *persistent petals*; *Canbya*, a curious little plant with the same anomaly (the last two really belonging to the Arizonian border of the interior desert region, although within California); *Platystigma*, including *Meconella*; *Platystemon*, with gynæcium singularly separating into its constituent carpels, so as to simulate a Ranunculaceous plant; *Dendromecon*, a shrub in an otherwise herbaceous family; and *Eschscholtzia*, the only genus which extends into the Great Basin, and the singular characters of which are familiar from the forms in common cultivation; add *Hunnemannia* from the Northern Mexican plateau. Next to the Sequoias, perhaps, these Papaveraceæ form the most characteristic note of the Californian flora.

FUMARIACEÆ.—Three genera, of which only the larger one, *Corydalis*, is amphigæan. Its species are of Eastern Asiatic rather than European types and relationship. *C. aurea* and its kindred forms, rather than species extend across the whole continent and to Japan; the striking species described as *C. Cascana*, of the western Rocky Mountains to the Sierra, appears to break into analogous forms which have recently been taken for species. *Dicentra*, peculiar to North America and the Japano-Himalayan floras, has perhaps a majority of American species. They belong wholly to wooded districts. One species crosses the whole continent along the northern border of our belt; in another case Pacific and Atlantic species hardly at all differ; the three or four others are peculiar. *Adlumia*, the remaining genus, is of a single Atlantic species.

CRUCIFERÆ.—For an order of over 170 genera and more than 2,200 species, North America, in her about 40 indigenous genera, none of over two dozen species, cannot be said to have a large share; and the exclusion of Arctic alpine forms reduces the number considerably. The Atlantic Cruciferæ are almost all European in type; *Leavenworthia* and *Warea* are the only peculiar genera. The eastern border of the plains has a local genus, *Selenia*, and there begin the characteristic genera *Streptanthus* and *Stanleya*, and species of *Vesicaria* multiply southward; the Rocky Mountains exhibit no characteristic type, unless it is *Physaria*, but the arid region beyond begins to share with California in the abundance of *Lepidium*, and in the several endemic genera, of which *Thysanocarpus* is the most characteristic. It is the Arizonian region that furnishes the American representatives of the Old Word genus *Biscutella*, the *Dithyræa* of Harvey.

CAPPARIDACEÆ.—Within the limits specified North America has no *Cappareæ*, but all the genera of *Cleomeæ* except two are indigenous and the greater part of them peculiar to it—all in the warmer parts, the number of species and types increasing southwestward, and extending into Mexico. The peculiar types, *Cristatella*, *Cleomella* (of several species), *Wislizenia*, and *Oxystylis*, are characteristic of the southern part of the central region.

RESEDACEÆ we exclude, believing *Oligomeris subulata* to have been a Spanish importation.

CISTACEÆ.—Two of the four genera of this more conspicuously oriental order, *Hudsonia* and *Lechea*, are peculiar to the Atlantic States, to which also three species of *Helianthemum* are indigenous, and there is one species on the coast of California. The order is wanting to the whole intervening portion of the continent.

VIOLACEÆ.—In species of *Viola* North America is as rich as the Old World, and the Pacific flora as rich as the Atlantic and with greater diversity of type; a few species common to each, but most of them peculiar. The central flora has hardly any except in the alpestrine region, and these few and of wide-spread species. A Mexican *Ionidium* reaches Arkansas and Arizona.

POLYGALACEÆ.—Represented by *Polygala.* The Atlantic flora is rich in species, all of them peculiar; the Pacific flora has only two, of a peculiar type. The Texano-Arizonian region has several, some of them Mexican, but from both the mountains and valleys of our belt the genus and the order are nearly absent.

KRAMERIACEÆ.—Should be separately reckoned, whatever view be taken of the affinity of the warm-American (chiefly Mexican) genus *Krameria.* One species reaches the plains of Arkansas, and has obtained a lodgment on the coast of Florida; two or three more extend along the Mexican frontier, but hardly infringe upon the region under consideration.

FRANKENIACEÆ.—Of a single genus, of warm temperate and subtropical coasts; has a Californian and Arizonian species; no Atlantic representative, but there is a quite peculiar species at the southeastern base of the Rocky Mountains.

CARYOPHYLLACEÆ.—The *Sileneæ* are feebly represented (by *Silene* only) in the Atlantic flora, yet by peculiar species; are nearly wanting from the Great Plains, scanty in the Rocky Mountains, but of increasing number and diversity as the Pacific flora is approached. The *Alsineæ,* moderately numerous, call for no remark, except for the increased number of species of *Arenaria* in the interior flora, most of them peculiar. *Stipulicida* is of a single strictly Atlantic species.

ILLECEBRACEÆ.—Nowhere very numerous, but most of the species and genera in the Old World. *Paronychia* is represented in the Atlantic flora; also in that of the plains and the eastern part of the Rocky Mountains. *Anychia* and *Siphonychia* are peculiar to the Atlantic flora; *Pentacæna* to that of the Pacific coast, extending to Chili. *Achyronychia,* a remarkable genus, of one species, belongs to the Arizonian rather than the California flora.

PORTULACACEÆ.—This may be regarded as an American order, although the Purslane has accompanied man all over the world. The single species of *Montia* has an immensely wide distribution over the cool parts of the world. One of *Claytonia* and several of *Calandrinia* are Australian, and two small genera are South African. So, as relates to distribution, it is a very suggestive order. The Atlantic States have only the two earliest known species of *Claytonia* and a *Talinum;* New Mexico has a peculiar genus (*Talinopsis*), too like an African one; the Rocky Mountain region has the characteristic and remarkable genus *Lewisia,* and more species of *Claytonia,* &c.; *Spraguea* and *Calyptridium* are peculiar to the whole country west of the Rocky Mountains proper; *Calandriniæ* are all western; and the Pacific flora contains most of the species of *Claytonia.*

ELATINACEÆ.—Two of our three species of *Elatine* occur in the Atlantic, Rocky Mountain, and Pacific floras; one is restricted to the latter. The Texan *Bergia* very sparingly occurs in the Great Basin and on the Pacific coast.

HYPERICACEÆ.—Represented by three genera, of which the two small ones, *Ascyrum* and *Elodes*, are peculiar to the Atlantic flora (except European relatives of the latter), which is rich in endemic species of *Hypericum*; the Pacific flora has three or four endemic species of the latter, the intervening region nothing of the order.

TERNSTRŒMIACEÆ.—This Eastern American and Eastern Asian order is represented only east of the Alleghanies, and by *Stuartia*, two species (the third in Japan); *Gordonia*, two species, and several hardly genuine species in tropical Asia.

MALVACEÆ.—This is one of the great and cosmopolitan orders, of which North America possesses a fair but not excessive representation. The species and forms here increase in number southwestward. Indigenous plants only being regarded, no genus is common to North America and Europe excepting *Lavatera*, represented by two or three singular and mostly shrubby species of the Californian coast. *Napæa* is strictly peculiar to the Atlantic flora, as also is the unique *Sida Napæa*. *Callirhoë* is peculiar to the borders of the same district and the plains adjacent. *Sidalcea* is peculiar to the Rocky Mountain and Californian floras. *Ingenhouzia* (which is *Thurberia*) belongs the Western Arizonian flora. *Malvastrum* and *Sphæralcea* (too near generically) are numerous in species on the plains and through the valleys of the Rocky Mountain region. *Kosteletzkya* is represented on the Atlantic coast, but most of the species are Mexican.

BOMBACEÆ.—*Fremontia Californica* belongs wholly to the forest district of the Sierra Nevada, and its only relative is *Cheirostemon*, the Hand-flower of Mexico.

TILIACEÆ.—Excepting one or two outlying plants on the southern borders, this order is represented only by the genus *Tilia*, in two species of the Atlantic States, which hardly cross the Mississippi.

LINACEÆ.—Three or four Atlantic species of *Linum*, as many more on the plains or Rocky Mountains, one species from the plains to the Pacific coast, and the same is an Old World species, or nearly so; and, moreover, in California and Oregon an unique group of seven species (*Hesperolinon*), in which the carpels are reduced from five to three, or even two.

ZYGOPHYLLACEÆ.—Leaving out the species of *Tribulus* or *Kallstrœmia* and the Texano-Arizonian representatives, among which *Fagonia Californica* should be ranked, notwithstanding the specific name, only the Creosote Bush remains, *Larrea Mexicana*, a shrub of the Mexican plateau, which has passed into or near the southern border of our belt all along from Texas to California.

GERANIACEÆ.—In the restricted sense, are few in North America, consisting only of a few species of *Geranium*; the eastern and western perennial ones different: a biennial species of a weedy character is scattered over the continent.

LIMNANTHEÆ.—Are exclusively North American: *Limnanthes*, of two or three species on the Pacific side, the reduced type *Flœrkea* on the Atlantic side also; all wanting to the Rocky Mountain flora.

OXALIDEÆ.—A very few species of *Oxalis*, one peculiar to the east and one to the west, one to the east and middle, and the *O. corniculata* both east and west.

BALSAMINEÆ.—Two species of *Impatiens* in the Atlantic States; none farther westward.

RUTACEÆ.—Mainly a tropical and subtropical order and not largely American, it is only to be noted that the *Ruteœ* are represented along the southern border by *Thamnosma*, a Texan species of which reaches the southern Rocky Mountains, and another belongs only to the southern border of the Great Basin. *Ptelea* extends quite across the continent, whether in one or in three species is uncertain; and two species of *Xanthoxylum* are restricted to the Atlantic border. *Cneoridium* is a little Californian shrub which rather belongs to this order. The American Simarubaceæ are south of our range.

CYRILLEÆ.—Two strictly Atlantic genera, one tropical American and a West Indian one, compose the group.

AQUIFOLIACEÆ are represented only in the Atlantic flora by a dozen species of *Ilex* and the peculiar monotypic genus *Nemopanthes*.

CELASTRACEÆ.—The single *Celastrus* is restricted to the Atlantic flora, which has also two species of *Euonymus;* the Pacific coast has one. *Pachystima* is a genus of two species, one common through the mountains from the Pacific to the Rocky Mountains, the other extremely local in the Alleghanies of Virginia.

RHAMNACEÆ.—Excluding the Texano-Arizonian forms and the subtropical of Florida, we are concerned only with *Rhamnus* and *Frangula*, one species of which crosses the continent northward, two Atlantic only, and two Pacific: *Sageretia* and *Berchemia*, each having one Atlantic coast species; and the great American genus *Ceanothus*. The original species and three others are restricted to the Atlantic flora; three are Mexican; but the rest, twenty or more species, belong to the Rocky Mountains, where there are few, and to the Pacific flora, where they are perhaps the most abundant and characteristic shrubs, forming a large part of the *chaparral*.

VITACEÆ.—*Ampelopsis* belongs to the Atlantic flora, but reaches the southern Rocky Mountains. *Vitis* has eight or nine species in the same flora, and is therefore more developed here than in any other part of the temperate zone. California has one species; the Rocky Mountains and their outlying districts none at all.

SAPINDACEÆ.—Most largely tropical, except that there is a *Sapindus* along the southern frontiers; are represented only by certain genera. Four species of *Æsculus* characterize the Atlantic flora; one, of a different type, the Pacific flora; and there is none between. Five species of *Acer* are peculiar to the Atlantic, two to the Pacific flora; one occurs only in the western Rocky Mountains; one is common to the latter and

3 G B

to the Pacific flora. *Negundo*, which is hardly distinct from *Acer*, has an Atlantic species extending to and through the Rocky Mountains; a second but closely related species takes its place in California. *Staphylea*, which affects only forest regions, has an Atlantic and a (local) Pacific species. *Glossopetalon* is peculiar to the intermediate dry region; the original species occurs on and beyond the southern borders of the Great Basin; a second one is on its northwestern border. *Ungnadia* of Texas is rather too far southwest to be well reckoned in the Atlantic forest flora, yet it belongs to it.

ANACARDIACEÆ.—Represented by the genus *Rhus*. The only species which extends across the continent is *R. aromatica*, in a peculiar western variety. *R. glabra*, the low Sumach, extends to and beyond the Rocky mountains. The common Sumach, the Poison Dogwood, and some others are wholly eastern, while *Rhus Toxicodendron* reaches the Rocky Mountains; on the Pacific side it is replaced by an equally poisonous and very similar species. Southern California has two other species of South American type.

LEGUMINOSÆ.—This being one of the very largest orders in most parts of the world, only characteristic features can be noted. The Atlantic flora is rich in genera, but poor, comparatively, in species; the Pacific is very poor in genera, but several of the genera are very numerous in species. The intervening region on the western side has the Californian character. They may be referred to under the suborders.

PAPILIONACEÆ.—The great preponderance of Pacific species is attributable mainly to the great development of four genera, viz: *Astragalus*, *Lupinus*, *Trifolium*, and *Hosackia*. The latter is the only purely American type of the four, though very near to the Old World genus *Lotus*, and, but for one species which has nearly reached the Atlantic seaboard, would be wholly western.

The only peculiar Pacific genus is *Pickeringia*, of a single species. There is no peculiar genus of the Rocky Mountain flora, *Olneya* being Arizonian. The exuberance of Atlantic genera is largely due to genera which are divided between the Eastern United States and Eastern Asia, such as *Wistaria*, *Apios*, *Amphicarpæa*, *Lespedeza*, *Cladrastis*, and to some exclusive genera, such as *Baptisia*, *Robinia*, *Petalostemon*; also to the absence toward the Pacific of genera which the Atlantic States share with Mexico and South America, such as *Tephrosia*, *Indigofera*, *Sesbania*, *Stylosanthes*, *Desmodium* (the largest Atlantic States genus), *Erythrina*, *Clitoria*, *Centrosema*, *Galactia*, *Rhynchosia*. Moreover, the botany of California should surrender its eleven species of *Dalea*, since they all properly belong to the Arizonian and Great Basin floras rather than to that of the Pacific region. It is a characteristic genus of the Mexican plateau and of its extension northward. *Astragalus*, feebly represented in the Atlantic States, and its appendage, *Oxytropis*, have their American headquarters in the plains and mountains of our interior region, under conditions not unlike those of Northern and Central Asia, where a great majority of the rest of the *Astragaleæ* flourish. *Amorpha* is shared by the Atlantic and Pacific floras. *Thermopsis*, with three local Atlantic species, one in the Rocky Mountains and two in California, has also Eastern Asian species.

CÆSALPINEÆ.—Excluding the Texano-Arizonian forms, the only Pacific representative is a single *Cercis*; the central region has none, except, perhaps, a *Hoffmanseggia* or two; while the Atlantic has a *Cercis* of its own, rising to the size of a forest tree, also stately trees in *Gymnocladus* and *Gleditschia* (two species), and of herbs a few species of *Cassia*.

MIMOSEÆ are in nearly similar case. Not one is truly to be reckoned in the Pacific flora or in the Rocky Mountain flora within our proper bounds, though several representatives appear a little farther south; but *Schrankia*, a *Mimosa*, a *Neptunia*, and two or three species of *Desmanthus* (all herbaceous) come within our limits on the ultra-Mississippian plains and barely enter the Atlantic flora. The shrubby or arboreal *Mimoseæ* (*Mimosa*, *Prosopis* in its two forms, *Acacia*, &c.) characterize the Texano-Mexican bordering district.

ROSACEÆ.—This important order has very characteristic North American genera. Unlike the preceding order, the western genera are more numerous than the eastern, and also about as numerous in species. Taken under their suborders or great groups—

CHRYSOBALANEÆ.—Are represented only on the Atlantic coast, and by a single *Chrysobalanus*, excluding, of course, the tropical one in Florida.

AMYGDALEÆ.—Occur in the Atlantic flora only under the true *Prunus*, *Padus*, *Cerasus*, and *Lauro-cerasus* sections, except that in Texas forms approaching *Amygdalus* occur. The Pacific flora has scanty representatives of the same types. The southern and western borders of the Great Basin are marked by two peculiar Amygdalus-like species, *Prunus Andersonii*, in which the exocarp falls from the stone in two valves like an almond, and *P. fasciculata*, on which Torrey founded a genus, *Emplectocladus*. Then, the Pacific coast has the curious and unique genus *Nuttallia*, Torr. & Gray, which is regularly pluricarpellary.

The true Rosaceæ have *Spiræa* in several types, *Neillia*, *Rubus*, *Geum*, *Fragaria*, *Potentilla*, *Agrimonia*, *Poterium*, and *Rosa*, in common over the continent, the species of *Potentilla* much increasing westward. Peculiar to the Atlantic flora are only *Neviusa* (of Japanese affinity), *Gillenia*, and *Dalibarda*; to the Pacific flora, *Chamæbatia*, which abounds over the western slope of the Sierra Nevada, and *Adenostoma*, which forms a large part of the *chaparral* or *chamisal* (the shrub is called "*Chamiso*") of the foot-hills and coast-ranges. Peculiar to the Rocky Mountain flora, mostly to the Great Basin and to its southward extension into Mexico, are *Coleogyne*, a single and very local shrub of the desert, *Coreania*, *Fallugia*. Peculiar, or nearly so, to the two western regions are *Cercocarpus* (with one Mexican species) and the two potentilliform genera or subgenera, *Horkelia* and *Ivesia*, the former of which might rather be ranked among the exclusively Pacific types. A single *Acæna* is one of the Chilian forms which has reached California. *Waldsteinia*, on the Atlantic side, is an Old World type.

POMEÆ.—The amphigæan genera or groups, *Cratægus, Malus, Sorbus, Amelanchier*, extend across the continent at the north, one *Sorbus* in the very same species; only *Cratægus* on the Atlantic side displays a considerable number of species; and the *Adenorachis* group is peculiar to the latter district. *Heteromeles*, of Asiatic type, is confined to the coast of California. *Peraphyllum* is a peculiar shrub of the western verge of the Great Basin.

CALYCANTHACEÆ.—Are all North American, except the single *Chimonanthus* of China; two species of *Calycanthus* peculiar to the Atlantic flora, one to that of California.

SAXIFRAGACEÆ.—An order hardly inferior to Rosaceæ in extent, in amount of diversification, and in wideness of distribution. Of the amphigæan types, headed by *Saxifraga*, it is unnecessary to discourse, except to mention that noble and most peculiar Californian species *S. peltata*. The peculiar North American genera are, on the Atlantic side, *Sullivantia* and *Decumaria ;* of the Rocky Mountain flora, *Jamesia*, and farther south, *Fendlera ;* of the Pacific flora, *Leptarrhena, Tolmiœa, Bolandra, Sucksdorfia, Carpenteria ;* of the Rocky Mountain and Pacific floras in common, *Tellima, Whipplea ;* of the Atlantic and Pacific floras, but not in the intervening, *Boykinia ;* of all three floras, *Heuchera ;* of all three northward, with extension merely into Northeastern Asia, *Tiarella* and *Mitella*, also, with intervening species farther south, *Philadelphus*. Then, *Astilbe, Hydrangea*, and *Itea* are genera strictly divided between the Atlantic flora and that of Himalaya-Japan. In *Lepuropetalon* we have the rare case of a species peculiar to the Atlantic and the Chilian floras, with no known connection. The genus *Ribes* assumes its maximum development and fullest diversification in North America and on its western borders. Even with the alpine species included, *Saxifraga* is comparatively weak in this country.

CRASSULACEÆ.—The amphigæan genera *Tillæa* and *Sedum* are not largely represented in North America. A Mexican group, *Echeveria*, extends well north along the Pacific coast, but is wanting in the interior. *Diamorpha*, an unique genus of a single species, allied to *Sedum*, is of the Atlantic flora. *Penthorum*, equally peculiar, is of a single species, restricted to the Atlantic States and to China and Japan.

DROSERACEÆ.—Appear to be absent from the whole Rocky Mountains, except in the cool regions far north ; the Pacific flora northward has the two common amphigæan species ; the Atlantic flora has four peculiar species, and also rejoices in *Dionæa*.

HAMAMELIDEÆ.—Are divided between Atlantic North America, South Africa, and Asia (to which most of the genera and species belong); our single *Hamamelis* does not cross the Mississippi; the monotypic *Fother-*

*gilla* hardly crosses the Alleghanies; the single *Liquidambar* is equally of eastern range, though it extends into and through Mexico.

HALORAGEÆ.—Are of small account. The amphigæan *Hippuris* and one or two of *Myriophyllum* extend across the continent northward; but *Proserpinaca*, of two species, is restricted to the Atlantic flora.

MELASTOMACEÆ.—*Rhexia* of the Atlantic flora alone represents this great typical order in a temperate climate.

LYTHRACEÆ.—Largely tropical or subtropical; two or three species of *Ammannia* and *Lythrum* are of wide distribution; and the Atlantic States have a *Cuphea* and a *Nesæa*, Eastern South American types. The peculiar genus *Didiplis* is nearly an aquatic *Ammannia*.

ONAGRACEÆ.—A largely American order. *Epilobium*, a cosmopolitan genus, is most diversified in the Pacific flora. *Clarkia*, *Boisduvalia*, *Eulobus*, *Eucharidium*, and *Heterogaura* are restricted to it; *Zauschneria*, *Gayophytum*, and the principal wealth of the great genus *Œnothera*, to the Rocky Mountain and Pacific region; *Gaura* and *Stenosiphon* mainly to the great plains east and southeast of the Rocky Mountains. *Ludwigia* and the diurnal yellow-flowered *Œnotheræ*, with clavate capsules, are Atlantic types. *Godetia* is one of the most characteristic of Pacific-coast genera, but also Chilian.

LOASACEÆ.—Are wholly American, with the odd exception of a South African genus of a single species. It is wanting from the Atlantic flora, but well represented in the Rocky Mountain and Pacific floras by various species of *Mentzelia*. The most showy vespertine species, *M. ornata* and *M. nuda*, are very characteristic on the plains between the Mississippi and the Rocky Mountains. *Eucnide* and *Petalonyx* are Texano-Arizonian genera.

TURNERACEÆ.—Tropical plants; one or two species of *Turnera* on the southern borders of the Atlantic flora.

PASSIFLORACEÆ.—Are equally unknown to the Rocky Mountain and Pacific floras. A very few species of *Passiflora* are indigenous to the Atlantic States, one extending as far north as Ohio.

CUCURBITACEÆ.—Are few in this country, and from the interior region within our proper limits they are absent. The true *Echinocystis* is peculiar to the Atlantic States; two or three species of *Megarrhiza* characterize the Pacific flora; perennial and tuberous rooted species of *Cucurbita* belong to the plains east of the Rocky Mountains (*C. perennis*) and through drier Texano-Arizonian regions.

DATISCACEÆ.—A single *Datisca* in California, far away from all its relatives.

CACTACEÆ.—Are abundant in and characteristic of the Rocky Mountain region, and still more of the Texano-Arizonian, as of the Mexican plateau. Two species of *Opuntia* extend along the Atlantic coast to New England. Twenty-six species are enumerated in the Botany of California, but a majority of them belong to the Arizonian district.

FICOIDEÆ.—Are extremely few and uninteresting. The early naturalization and great abundance of *Mesembrianthemum* on the coast of California is somewhat wonderful.

UMBELLIFERÆ.—This great order of over 150 genera is not notably large in North America. The number of genera in the Atlantic and the Pacific floras is about the same, but the species of the latter are much more numerous, and the interior region is equally well supplied. The largest western genera are *Cymopterus* and *Peucedanum*, the former peculiar to the region. *Phellopterus*, a plant of the northern Pacific sea-coast, is also on the coast of Japan. *Angelica Gmelini* is common to the two, also to the mountains and the sea-shore of Northern New England. *Cryptotænia* of the Atlantic flora is identically the same in Japan. *Osmorrhiza* consists of two Atlantic species, two Rocky Mountain and Pacific, and one of Japan, all closely related. *Crantzia lineata*, a little plant of the Atlantic States seaboard, occurs on the border of Mexico and in South America, and again on the seaboard of Chili and Patagonia, on the Falkland Islands, and even in New Zealand and Australia.

ARALIACEÆ.—Are few in North America, but interesting for distribution. Apparently there are none at all in the whole Rocky Mountain region, except one in Southern New Mexico. There are only two in the Pacific flora; one of them is very close to the Atlantic *Aralia racemosa* and is Californian; the other, *Fatsia horrida*, forms an undergrowth in the Coniferous woods of the coast farther north, and is also in the northern part of Japan. The Atlantic flora contains *Aralia spinosa*, the *A. racemosa* already mentioned, *A. hispida*, *A. quinquefolia*, the American Ginseng, and *A. trifolia*. Nearly all of these have close representatives in the Northeastern Asian (and Himalayan) region and not elsewhere.

CORNACEÆ.—Are of equally interesting distribution. Of the ordinary Cornels, four Pacific species are thought to be distinct from the seven of the Atlantic flora, although the characters are not very well made out, and they meet more or less in the Rocky Mountains. Then, California only has a species (*C. sessilis*), of the European and Japanese *C. mas* type. *C. florida* of the Atlantic flora has a more showy representative in *C. Nuttallii* of the Pacific forest, and less close relatives in Eastern Asia. The herbaceous *C. Canadensis* crosses the continent at the north, and in Japan meets the allied *C. Suecica*. *Nyssa*, of the Atlantic flora, has congeners in the mountains of Asia, while *Garrya* of the Pacific flora has them in the Texano-Mexican region and the West Indies.

CAPRIFOLIACEÆ.—Of the amphigæan genera there is little to remark, except the considerable development of *Viburnum* in the Atlantic flora in species strictly cognate if not sometimes identical with those of Japan; their absence from the Rocky Mountains, except well northward, where two cross to the northwest coast; and the occurrence on the Pacific side of only one endemic species. *Symphoricarpus*, a wholly American genus, has one or two species common to all three floras, one or two peculiar to each, in the central region a peculiar Mexican type. *Triosteum* is confined to the Atlantic flora and to Northeastern Asia, with the Himalaya.

RUBIACEÆ.—This vast order of over 300 genera and 4,000 species forms an insignificant feature in North America, and in the northern temperate zone throughout. But the poverty of the Rocky Mountain and the Pacific floras is extreme. There are some species of *Galium* in all, and *Cephalanthus* is on both sides of the continent and of southern extension. Besides, the Pacific flora has only the peculiar monotypic genus *Kelloggia*, with no near relative in the northern hemisphere. The Atlantic flora nearly monopolizes the genuine species of *Houstonia*, and its specially characteristic genus is *Mitchella*, which is repeated in a very similar species in Japan.

VALERIANACEÆ.—A small family, is here unimportant. The only peculiar genus is *Plectritis* of the Pacific coast and that of Chili.

COMPOSITÆ.—No detailed analysis can be expected here of the distribution of an order which is thought to make up one-tenth of flowering plants and which composes a still larger proportion of those of North America. Yet a few points may be brought to view, taking the tribes separately.

VERNONIACEÆ.—Are known only in the Atlantic region, the principal genus, *Vernonia*, however, extending over the prairie border of the plains. *Stokesia* is one of those strictly peculiar genera of a single species with which the Atlantic flora abounds.

EUPATORIACEÆ.—This is almost an American tribe, the maximum in South America, the minimum in our Pacific Territory, which has only four or five species. But into the Rocky Mountains and the Great Basin extends, more largely than into the Pacific flora, the genus *Brickellia*, founded on an outlying species of the Atlantic flora, yet mainly a Texano-Mexican genus. But the Atlantic flora is better supplied, and with peculiar genera, viz, *Sclerolepis, Trilisia, Carphephorus* (the South California species is hardly congeneric), the fine and rather large genus *Liatris*, which, however, reaches nearly to the Rocky Mountains and into Mexico, and *Kuhnia*, which is in the same case. *Garberia* of Florida, taken from *Liatris*, is too southern to be properly counted. The great genus *Eupatorium* is also well represented on the Atlantic side, and here only is the northern extension, in a single species, of the huge South American genus *Mikania*.

ASTEROIDEÆ.—Are eminently American, and in no other single district are they so numerous as in the belt across the continent which is under consideration. *Aster, Solidago*, and *Bigelovia* are the great genera; *Aplopappus, Chrysopsis, Erigeron*, and *Townsendia* are next in importance. About four-fifths of the *Asters* and *Solidagos* belong to the Atlantic flora, with some extension into the plains beyond, and there also are more species and forms (but fewer individuals) of *Chrysopsis; the amphigen genus *Erigeron* has its fullest development and diversification in our western regions; *Aplopappus* is divided between our Rocky Mountain flora (with southward extension and into that of the Pacific) and that of Chili. *Townsendia* and *Bigelovia* are the most characteristic genera of the whole

Rocky Mountain region, although a few species of the latter reach the Pacific, while the original one belongs to the Atlantic coast. *Grindelia* and *Gutierrezia* are equally characteristic over the plains and quite over to the Pacific, and both are sparingly represented in extratropical South America. *Lessingia, Corethrogyne,* and *Pentachæta* are peculiarly Californian. *Boltonia* and the *Bellis integrifolia* are peculiarly Atlantic. *Baccharis,* with an immense development in South America and Mexico, has penetrated northward on both coasts to about latitude 41°, eastward in a single, westward in very few species.

INULOIDEÆ.—Are sparingly represented in America, and mostly in the Gnaphalineous type. They are particularly few in the Atlantic flora, and increase in number and diversification westward.

HELIANTHOIDEÆ.—On the contrary, are mostly American, and largely North American. Here are almost all the true species of *Helianthus,* the perennials mainly Atlantic, the annuals more western. The Atlantic flora is characterized by *Silphium, Chrysogonum, Tetragonotheca, Echinacea,* and the greater part of *Rudbeckia* and *Coreopsis,* and it alone has a *Heliopsis;* the eastern plains have *Thelesperma* (more developed farther south, and reproduced in Buenos Ayres!), *Engelmannia,* most of *Berlandiera,* &c.; the Rocky Mountains, *Balsamorrhiza, Wyethia, Helianthella,* &c., which they share with the Pacific flora; the latter reproduces the Coreopsoid type in *Leptosyne* and *Pugiopappus.*

GALINSOGEÆ and MADIEÆ.—Being exclusively American (and Hawaiian), and more related to the following than to the preceding tribe, deserve separate mention. *Baldwinia* and *Marshallia* are peculiar to the Atlantic flora; *Blepharipappus* to the Pacific. The rest are *Madieæ,* and are specially characteristic of our Pacific flora—are peculiar to it, indeed, except for the two Hawaiian Island genera, for the extension of the common *Madia* into Chili, and for the eastward extension of some species into the plains. *Madia, Layia,* and *Hemizonia,* in numerous species, many of them showy, are predominant Compositæ in California.

HELENIOIDEÆ (including the groups assigned to this tribe by Bentham).—Are specially American, are few in the Atlantic flora (where the few representatives are all of western types), are more numerous and characteristic in and towards the Rocky Mountains, while beyond them, as well as south of them and on the Pacific coast, they attain their fullest development. We will not enumerate the numerous mostly endemic genera.

ANTHEMIDEÆ.—Chiefly of the Old World; would be most insignificant in North America except for the number of naturalized weeds and for the remarkable development of species and individuals of *Artemisia,* especially of those which compose the Sage-brush on either side of the Rocky Mountains. These have already been spoken of. For anything like this development, as well as of the Chenopodiaceæ, which accompany the Wormwoods, only corresponding parts of Northern Asia can be looked to.

SENECIONIDEÆ.—Somewhat equally distributed over the world; offer little for remark. There is no peculiar type in the Atlantic flora nor east of the Rocky Mountains, but beyond them *Tetradymia* and *Psathyrotes* are truly characteristic of the Great Basin; *Raillardella* (the relatives of which are only in the Sandwich or Hawaiian Islands) is peculiar to the high Sierra Nevada, and *Luina* to the Pacific coast ranges. Western North America is, morever, the headquarters of *Arnica*.

CYNAROIDEÆ.—Are restricted to *Cnicus*, of which the Atlantic States, the Rocky Mountains and their accessory western ranges, and the Pacific side of the continent have about an equal and a moderate number of species (more or less peculiar), and the showy *Centaurea Americana*, now well known in cultivation, which inhabits the plains of Arkansas and Texas.

MUTISIACEÆ (including all the *Bilabiatiflora* of De Candolle).—Affect the southern hemisphere, but come into a temperate region both in North America and Asia. In the former most are of the Texano-Arizonian district—*Leria, Trixis, Perezia*—and are outliers of the Mexican flora ; but one of the latter genus fairly reaches California, and the original *Chaptalia* is of the Atlantic Southern States.

CICHORACEÆ, or the *Liguliflora*.—A very moderate number of the sixty genera are indigenous to North America. *Apogon, Krigia,* and *Cynthia* are peculiar to the Atlantic flora or its borders, *Pyrrhopappus* to this and the nearer parts of Mexico, and *Nabalus* has only one extraneous northwestern species; but the open western country nourishes the greater part of our representatives of this tribe. From the plains to the Pacific spreads the genus *Troximon*, accompanied by *Lygodesmia* and *Stephanomeria*, and even by *Malacothrix; Glyptopleura, Anisocoma,* and mainly *Calycoseris* are peculiar types in the Great Basin ; and fifteen species of *Malacothrix* are peculiar, or nearly so, to the Pacific flora, which has also *Rafinesquia, Aparyidium,* and *Phalacroseris.* The paucity of the large and difficult Old World genus *Hieracium* in America is a wonder and a relief to botanists.

LOBELIACEÆ.—*Lobelia* is essentially wanting from the Pacific and the Rocky Mountain floras, but well represented in that of the Atlantic. Instead, the Pacific flora is characterized by four peculiar genera, *Downingia, Howellia* (an aquatic plant of Oregon), *Palmerella,* and the curious *Nemacladus.* It has also a peculiar *Laurentia,* which extends eastward to the Rocky Mountains, where it is the only representative of the family.

CAMPANULACEÆ.—Are not numerous; but *Campanula* has a few representatives in all three floras (in the interior only on the mountains); *Specularia* has fewer; and two genera of single species, *Githopsis* and *Heterocodon,* are peculiar to the Pacific flora.

ERICACEÆ.—This important order needs to be considered under its suborders.

VACCINEÆ.—In the northern hemisphere affect the eastern side of continents. The five species of *Gaylussacia* (Huckleberries), and the dozen or more eastern endemic species of *Vaccinium*, as also the peculiar genus *Chiogenes*, sparingly enter even the eastern part of the Mississippi Valley. Only amphigæan types occur in the Rocky Mountains and in the alpine or alpestrine region. The moister parts of the Pacific coast nourish two or three species of *Vaccinium*, but no other forms; yet all the Atlantic types, except *Gaylussacia*, occur again in Northeastern Asia.

ERICINEÆ.—In North America are not unequally divided between the Atlantic and Pacific floras; but the interior region has very few, not one peculiar, and none except upon high mountains or of equivalent northern range. The Pacific flora is remarkable for having an *Arbutus* and ten species of *Arctostaphylos* of the Mexican type, for its solitary *Leucothoë* far away from congeners, its shrubby *Gaultheria*, and its species of *Bryanthus;* also for the peculiar *Ledum* which it shares with the Northern Rocky Mountains. It has one peculiar genus, *Cladothamnus.* The specially Atlantic Ericineous genera are *Epigœa* (yet with a Japanese counterpart), *Oxydendrum, Kalmia, Leiophyllum,* and *Elliottia*, this shared with Japan. This flora is particularly rich in *Andromedeæ* of eight or nine types, and here alone in the temperate zone we find a *Bejaria.* Only the counterpart Asiatic region excels it in *Rhododendron* and *Azalea;* yet the Pacific flora has three or four fine representatives of these. *Menziesia* in one species occurs over the breadth of the continent at the north, adding a second species on the way; thence to Japan, where there are more.

PYROLINEÆ (including *Clethra* as the type of a peculiar tribe).—The two species of the latter genus are characteristic in the Atlantic flora; they are not found west even of the Alleghanies, to which one of them is restricted. North America is the headquarters of *Pyrola* and the related genera, having nearly all the known species; and the western floras possess their full share.

MONOTROPEÆ.—Also are strikingly American, notwithstanding the wide distribution of the typical *Monotropa* from South America to Himalaya, and to Europe of *Hypopitys.* All the genera and species, except one in Himalaya, occur in North America, and all but the peculiar Atlantic genus *Schweinitzia* are in the Pacific flora, to which half the genera are peculiar.

LENNOACEÆ —A Mexican group of three genera, having the habit of *Monotropeæ;* has one genus, *Pholisma*, on the coast of California, and another very singular one, *Ammobroma*, Torr., beyond its borders at the head of the Gulf of California.

DIAPENSIACEÆ, upon which we have elsewhere dilated, consist of the arctic-alpine *Diapensia Lapponica* and a congener in Himalaya, of two monotypic genera in the Atlantic United States (*Pyxidanthera* and *Galax*), of another (*Shortia*) divided between the Alleghanies (where it is apparently verging to extinction) and Japan, of a related genus in the latter country, and of another in Tibet. From our western floras it is totally absent.

PLUMBAGINACEÆ.—In this country very few, and confined to the sea-coasts; are not noteworthy.

PRIMULACEÆ.—Need little mention, most of the genera being amphigæan and widely distributed over the country, although few in species, many of them alpine or alpestrine. The most peculiar genus, *Dodecatheon*, spans the continent in very various forms, which seem to be connected into one species. The true species of *Lysimachia* are only on the Atlantic side, and so mainly is the peculiar genus *Steironema*, although the commonest species extends northward to the Pacific.

SAPOTACEÆ.—This is one of several orders which, although mainly tropical, have temperate representatives in the Atlantic United States, where there are at least three species of *Bumelia*.

EBENACEÆ.—Are in similar case. *Diospyros Virginiana*, our Persimmon, extends north to latitude 41°, and barely crosses the Mississippi. A Texan species lies beyond our line. Westward the order is wanting.

STYRACACEÆ.—Are found on both sides of the continent, but not at all in the intermediate regions. The order is one of those that affect the eastern side of continents. Accordingly, the Atlantic flora has three genera (*Symplocos, Halesia, Styrax*) and eight species; the Pacific flora only a single *Styrax*.

OLEACEÆ.—Are fairly well represented in the Atlantic flora by six or seven species of *Fraxinus*, a few of *Forestiera*, a *Chionanthus*, and an *Osmanthus*; two species of *Fraxinus* are the sole representatives in the Pacific flora. The wide intervening region has none except a *Fraxinus*, with simple leaves, on the southern border, where also flourish one or two species of *Forestiera* and of the Texano-Mexican genus *Menodora*.

APOCYNACEÆ.—The two species of *Apocynum* make a part of all three floras; the Pacific has a peculiar genus, *Cycladenia*; the Atlantic, a plant referred to the Northeastern Asian genus *Trachelospermum*, and *Amsonia* (which is also Japanese), the latter reaching the southern borders of the Great Basin.

ASCLEPIADACEÆ.—Most of *Asclepias* is North American, and the species, as to number, are not very unequally divided between the three floras, at least if New Mexico and Arizona be taken into the account. This southern frontier and the country beyond is rather rich in the order. The Pacific flora has three species nearly related to *Asclepias*; one of them is made the type of a peculiar genus, *Schizonotus*, the other two are referred to the chiefly African genus *Gomphocarpus*. The Atlantic flora divides with that of the plains up to the Rocky Mountains the genera *Acerates* and *Asclepiodora*, with tropical parts of America the genus *Enslenia*, and is also rich in *Gonolobus*; and it monopolizes the genera *Podostigma* and *Amanthesis*.

LOGANIACEÆ.—As our species of *Buddleia* and the genus *Emorya* belong to the Texano-Arizonian region, it may be said that this order is here restricted to the Atlantic flora. This divides *Gelsemium* with Eastern Asia, *Spigelia* and *Polypremum* with tropical America, *Mitreola* with both.

GENTIANACEÆ.—The Gentians. generally most numerous in mountain districts, preponderate in our western floras; yet the Atlantic States do not lack species. The amphigæan genus *Erythrea* is finely represented in the Pacific flora and in the Texano-Arizonian region, sparingly in the Rocky Mountain region, while in the Atlantic States there is probably no indigenous species north and east of Arkansas. *Microcala* has probably reached California from South America. *Menyanthes trifoliata* is all around the northern part of the temperate zone. *M. cristagalli* is one of the few plants which the Pacific flora shares with that of Japan. The two species of *Limnanthemum* are strictly Atlantic, and are connected with tropical species of the eastern side of the continent. *Halenia* is at the same time a high-northern and an Andean genus. *Swertia* is absent from the Atlantic side of the continent. As to the peculiarly American genera, the finest is *Frasera*, with one Atlantic species, and a few others both of the Rocky Mountains and of the Pacific side of the continent. *Eustoma* reaches from the Texano-Arizonian region just within our border over to the eastern border of the plains. *Sabbatia*, of thirteen species, *Bartonia*. and *Obolaria* are wholly peculiar to the Atlantic flora.

POLEMONIACEÆ.—Although not wholly absent from Europe and Northern Asia, compose a truly characteristic American order, and, although half the genera are Mexican and South American, at least nine-tenths of the species must belong to the United States. Of these, an equally large proportion adorn the western regions, whether the mountains, the valleys, or the plains. under the various forms of *Gilia*, *Collomia*, and *Phlox*. Yet, to the Atlantic States belong the herbaceous perennial species of the latter genus, which have longest been known to botanists.

HYDROPHYLLACEÆ.—This is more strictly an American, and even more predominantly a Western North American, order than the preceding. A very large part of our species and forms inhabit the Rocky Mountain region, chiefly its plains and valleys, and fewest the Atlantic region. No genus is restricted to the latter, though into it only extends the southern *Hydrolea* ; into the lower parts of the intermediate regions extends the mainly Texano-Mexican genus *Nama* ; to it belongs *Conanthus*, *Tricardia*, and essentially *Lemmonia* ; to it and to the Pacific flora belong *Emmenanthe*, *Hesperochiron*, *Eriodictyon* ; to the Pacific flora alone belong *Draperia* and *Romanzoffia*.

BORRAGINACEÆ.—This is a larger order, and is found all over the world. The tribes or suborders other than the *Borrageæ* hardly come at all within our limits, excepting two or three species of *Heliotropium*, one of which is very characteristic of the plains east of the Rocky Mountains (viz. *H. convolvulaceum*, the *Euploca* of Nuttall, and it has also been found in the Great Basin), and excepting the *Tiquilia* section of *Coldenia*, which extends to the northwestern verge of the interior woodless region. The genera and species are few in the Atlantic flora. Its only characteristic genus is *Onosmodium*; the yellow-flowered and showy *Lithosperma* of the section *Batschia* it shares with the plains. The great genus of the whole Rocky Mountain flora, though shared with the Pacific, is *Eritrichium*; the characteristic genus of the Pacific flora, of which its neighbor takes a part, is *Amsinckia*. *Mertensia* has most of its species in the Rocky Mountains and their accessories, yet the finest of them is *M. Virginica*, peculiar to the Atlantic States. *Pectocarya* may have been brought from Chili to California. Some peculiar genera of the Arizonian flora are hardly within our scope.

CONVOLVULACEÆ.—There are no peculiar genera in North America, and nothing notable in distribution. There are many more Atlantic than Pacific species.

SOLANACEÆ.—As to truly indigenous species, are few north and east of Texas, and not numerous through the western portions of the country. *Physalis* is the largest genus. The only peculiar genera are *Chamæsaracha* and the very little known *Oryctes*, neither of salient character, both of the interior region. Into the southern part of the Rocky Mountains extend from Mexico two species or forms of the Potato type.

SCROPHULARIACEÆ.—North America has 37 indigenous genera of this very large order, several of them numerous in species. They are fewest in the Atlantic flora, which yet has some peculiar genera, and it is noteworthy that only one of them (*Schwalbea*) is of near affinity to Japano-Himalayan types. Throughout, the types which are not distinctively American are rather European, *Mimulus*, however, being an exception. Thus, in California there is a remarkable development of the genus *Antirrhinum*. Of the several tribes, there is one which is particularly characteristic of the Atlantic flora, namely, that which contains *Gerardia* (of over 20 species), and is augmented by *Macranthera, Seymeria*, and *Buchnera*. Some species abound on the eastern part of the plains, but none reach the Rocky Mountains or appear in the country beyond them. Of genera which are sparingly represented in the Atlantic flora or near its borders, and are in fuller strength westward, the more characteristic are *Collinsia*, and the great genus *Pentstemon*, with about 4 species at the east and nearly 40 in the Pacific flora; *Mimulus*, with 3 Atlantic and at least 23 Pacific species; *Synthyris; Castelleia*, with 3 or 4 Atlantic and about 20 western species; *Orthocarpus* with one species on the northeastern plains and 24 in the western floras, chiefly on the Pacific side, while its relatives in *Cordylanthus* add half as many more. So *Pedicularis*, with only 2 Atlantic species, increases westward to over 20.

OROBANCHACEÆ.—The four North American genera are wholly distinct from the European, and from the Asian also, except for an Eastern Asian species of *Boschniakia*. Here also, although two of the genera are wholly Atlantic and one is divided (*Aphyllon*), the Pacific species are more than twice the number of the Atlantic.

LENTIBULACEÆ.—Both *Utricularia* and *Pinguicula* are of good number and diversity in the Atlantic flora, are nearly absent from the Rocky Mountain flora, and are very few on the Pacific side.

BIGNONIACEÆ.—For a mainly tropical order, are pretty well represented in the Atlantic flora by four species belonging to three genera (and the most distinct genus, *Catalpa*, also in Japan and Northern China), but would be wholly absent from the western floras except for a Mexican shrub (*Chilopsis*) which reaches the southern borders of the Great Basin.

PEDALIACEÆ.—Are sparingly represented in the Texano-Arizonian region, but probably are not indigenous to the north of it.

ACANTHACEÆ.—An immense tropical and subtropical order, but probably without a single representative in the Rocky Mountain or Pacific floras within our limits, yet with several in the Texano-Arizonian district. But the Atlantic flora has an *Elytraria* and *Hygrophila*, one or two species of *Calophanes*, as many of *Ruellia* and of *Dianthera*, a *Dicliptera*, and a plant of a peculiar genus, *Gatesia*.

VERBENACEÆ.—Of the eleven genera enumerated in the flora of North America, only four are of such northern range as to come within our limits. *Verbena* and *Lippia* enter into all three floras. *Callicarpa* and *Phryma* are restricted to the Atlantic flora and to a solitary species. Both the latter are Eastern Asian, the *Phryma* in the same species.

LABIATÆ.—A large and important order, but after excluding the naturalized plants and those which range south of the present survey, neither the American species nor the genera are particularly numerous, nor is their distribution such as to call for much remark. They are most conspicuous in the Pacific forest in the Rocky Mountain region, most diversified in genera in the Atlantic States. Of the North American types, *Physostegia*, *Lophanthus*, *Pycnanthemum*, and *Trichostema* are common to both sides of the continent, the latter most largely on the Pacific; the latter numerously on the Atlantic side, with a single Californian species far away from its congeners. The peculiar Atlantic genera are *Isanthus*, *Cunila*, *Collinsonia*, *Conradina*, *Ceranthera*, *Blephilia*, *Monarda* (which extends into the Rocky Mountains), *Brazoria*, *Macbridea*, *Synandra*. The Pacific peculiar genera are only *Monardella*, *Pogogyne*, *Acanthomintha*, *Audibertia*, the first and the last extending eastward to the Rocky Mountains in single species. *Hedeoma* is a remaining characteristic genus, with headquarters in the Texano-Mexican district, extending over the eastern plains, and one species to the Atlantic. The great genus *Salvia* is meager on both sides of the continent, almost absent from the interior, except on the eastern plains toward the south, but fairly numerous in species throughout the Texano-Arizonian region.

PLANTAGINACEÆ.—Are few in species. *Plantago Patagonica*, which abounds on the plains and on the Pacific coast southward, is very polymorphous and of immense geographical range. It is worth noting here that the other genus, *Littorella*, till now supposed to be wholly European, has been detected at three or four stations within and near the northern borders of the United States.

NYCTAGINACEÆ.—Are essentially absent from the Atlantic flora, abundant in the Texano-Arizonian; are represented by *Oxybaphus* on the plains east of the Rocky Mountains and by *Abronia* beyond them; also by *Quamoclidion* or *Mirabilis* with several-flowered calciform involucre. The Great Basin has a peculiar genus, *Hermidium* of S. Watson, allied to *Bougainvillæa* of South America, but herbaceous.

AMARANTACEÆ (weeds excluded).—Are chiefly of the Rocky Mountain region in its warmer and drier parts. *Acnida*, however, is more eastern.

CHENOPODIACEÆ.—Are of similar distribution, but far more numerous and diverse. They are the most characteristic and abundant of the plants of the dry interior region, as has been elsewhere stated, and they naturally extend into the Pacific flora more than into the Atlantic. *Atriplex* is the great genus. *Grayia* and *Sarcobatus* are the endemic shrubby genera. *Spirostachys* is of an extratropical South American type. *Cycloloma* and *Suckleya* are herbs peculiar to the eastern plains.

PHYTOLACCACEÆ.—Are represented only in the Atlantic flora, and by a single *Phytolacca*, *Ririna* belonging farther south.

POLYGONACEÆ.—The genuine *Polygoneæ* on the Atlantic and Pacific sides by *Polygonum* and *Rumex*, and by *Polygonella* in the southern part of the former; and there are a few in the interior, where *Rumex venosus* is a characteristic plant. But the most characteristic plants of the two western floras, and the most numerous in species, if not in individuals, are the *Eriogoneæ*. The genus *Eriogonum*, founded at the beginning of the century upon the single-known and still the only Atlantic species, now comprises nearly 100 species in our western floras, and the subsidiary genera (*Oxytheca*, *Centrostegia*, *Chorizanthe*, *Nemacaulis*, *Hollisteria*, and *Lastarreia*, all mainly Californian, and three of them also Chilian) about three score more. *Pterostegia*, of California, proves to be most related to the arctic-alpine *Kœnigia*. Another type is represented in the southern part of the Atlantic flora by the peculiar genus *Brunnichia*.

PODOSTEMACEÆ.—Aquatic plants of tropical or subtropical rivers, mostly of the southern hemisphere. A single *Podostemon*, on which the genus and order were founded, belongs to the Atlantic United States. Its congeners are all in Brazil, Madagascar, and India!

ARISTOLOCHIACEÆ.—Absent from the whole intermediate region, there are three species of *Asarum* in the Atlantic and three others in the Pacific flora; three of *Aristolochia* in the former and one in the latter.

PIPERACEÆ, tribe *Saurureæ*.—A *Saururus* in the Atlantic flora, the only other one Chino-Japanese; a *Houttuynia* (if not a good genus, *Anemiopsis*) in California and thence to Mexico; its relatives also East African.

LAURACEÆ.—Mainly tropical or subtropical all around the world, yet there are three genera in the Atlantic flora (one, *Sassafras*, a fine tree, and all of Asiatic affinities) and a peculiar one in California.

THYMELÆACEÆ.—Most developed in the southern hemisphere. In North America is only *Dirca*, one species in the Atlantic flora, the other, very local, in the Californian.

ELÆAGNACEÆ.—Two of the three genera of this little order are North American. The two species of *Shepherdia* nearly traverse the continent at the north, and a third species has been discovered on the southern rim of the Great Basin. An *Elæagnus* belongs to Rocky Mountain region.

LORANTHACEÆ.—Are represented by two genera, allied to *Viscum*. *Phoradendron* is peculiar to America. The common species in some its of forms traverses the continent; another belongs to the Californian district and adjacent parts; the others are more southern. *Arceuthobium* is amphigæan, of three or four American species, mostly Pacific or southern, one sparingly represented in the Northern Atlantic States.

SANTALACEÆ.—Are most largely of the southern hemisphere. The distribution of our four genera is interesting. *Comandra* consists of a European species, two North American ones, which traverse the continent northward, and a fourth, which belongs mainly to the Rocky Mountain region southward. *Buckleya* consists of an Atlantic (Alleghanian) species and one in Japan; *Darbya* of a single and local Atlantic species, of some ambiguity, because the female plant is unknown; *Pyrularia* of an Alleghanian species and a Himalayan.

EUPHORBIACEÆ.—An immense order of 3,000 species and, at the least, 200 genera. The world-wide and prolific genus *Euphorbia* is very moderately represented in the Atlantic flora, sparingly in the Pacific, numerously in the drier parts of the intermediate country, especially southward. The other large and non-peculiar genera are mainly southern in range. Peculiar genera are very few—*Eremocarpus* in the Pacific flora; *Crotonopsis* in the Atlantic. Of the *Buxineæ*, there is *Simmondsia* on the Californian coast, of no near affinity; *Pachysandra*, in the Alleghanies, which has a congener in Japan.

EMPETRACEÆ.—Have all three genera in the Atlantic flora, and not elsewhere—*Empetrum* alpine and northern; *Corema* on the coast of the United States, the other species on the opposite Atlantic coast in Portugal; *Ceratiola* in the Southern Atlantic States.

CERATOPHYLLEÆ.—Probably of a single species, amphigæan, both Atlantic and Pacific.

URTICACEÆ.—Taken in the large sense, may be referred to under their suborders.

URTICEÆ.—Are few on either side of the continent, nearly absent from the Rocky Mountains and Great Basin, an *Urtica* or two, and the same of *Parietaria; Hesperocnide* is divided between California and the Hawaiian Islands; *Laportea*, of the Atlantic States, has its congeners mainly in Eastern Asia. The solitary North American *Pilea* is confined to the Atlantic States, and the same of *Bœhmeria*.

ULMACEÆ.—There are four fine Elm trees in the Atlantic flora, and one farther southwest, also the *Planera*; none of these in the Rocky Mountain or the Pacific floras; *Celtis*, either a form of the common eastern or a peculiar species, extends into the Rocky Mountains and even to Oregon.

CANNABINEÆ.—The common Hop of the Old World is indigenous in the Atlantic States and in the Rocky Mountains; the other species is Chino-Japanese.

MOREÆ.—*Morus rubra* is of the Atlantic States, extending far southward and thence westward, perhaps passing into a small-leaved species. *Maclura aurantiaca*, the Osage Orange, belongs to the northwestern borders of the Atlantic district. None in the western floras.

PLATANACEÆ.—There is one Atlantic and one Californian *Platanus*; but none intervening, except on the Mexican borders.

LEITNERIEÆ.—The anomalous *Leitneria*, of Florida, is of a single species, of wholly obscure affinity.

JUGLANDACEÆ.—*Juglans cinerea* and *J. nigra* or the Walnut trees of the Atlantic flora, *J. California* of the Pacific; *Carya* is of seven species, restricted to the Atlantic flora.

CUPULIFERÆ.—Are most fully represented in the Atlantic flora, are prominent in the Pacific flora, but are wanting in the whole interior region, excepting a Scrub Oak or two on the Rocky Mountains and their accessories. There are twenty-one Oaks, two Chestnuts, and a Beech in the Atlantic flora; nine Oaks and a *Castanopsis* in the Pacific flora; one Oak in the Rocky Mountain flora, or perhaps more than one; and two or three others in the district between it and Mexico.

CORYLACEÆ.—An *Ostrya* and a *Carpinus* and two species of *Corylus* represent this group in the Atlantic flora. The two western floras want all but one of the latter, which traverses the continent.

BETULACEÆ.—Are represented in the Atlantic flora by seven Birches and three Alders. One of the smaller Birches and perhaps one of the Alders, extends over to the Pacific flora, along with another Rocky Mountain Birch, and two or three Alders are added.

MYRICACEÆ.—The amphigæan *Myrica Gale* is of the Atlantic flora; one very like it in the Pacific. Of the Bayberry *Myricæ*, there are one or two on the Atlantic, and another on the Pacific coast. The *Comptonia* is peculiar to the Atlantic flora.

SALICINEÆ.—There are about fifteen Willows indigenous to the Atlantic States, nineteen in the Californian flora, very few of them identical; the Rocky Mountains have a few of these and one or two more of alpine type. There are six Poplars in the Atlantic States; three or four in California and Oregon; one or two in the intermediate country, besides *P. tremuloides*, which, passing along the mountains, is common to all three floras.

The *Gymnospermeæ* may best be exhibited under the particular groups.

GNETACEÆ.—*Ephedra*, the only extratropical genus, is absent from

4 G B

the Atlantic flora, has three or four species in the Texano-Arizonian region, two of which enter the Great Basin, and one belongs to the southern part of California.

TAXINEÆ are absent from the Rocky Mountain flora. The Atlantic flora has the depressed *Taxus Canadensis* at the north, and an upright arborescent and perhaps peculiar species in the northern part of Florida. There is a similar one in the woods of the Pacific side of the continent. The Atlantic flora possesses the original *Torreya;* California another; the two remaining species are of Northeastern Asia.

CUPRESSINEÆ.—The amphigæan *Juniperus communis* traverses the continent at the north; and a prostrate form of *J. Sabina* probably does the same; also *J. Virginiana*, the eastern Red Cedar. But on a southern range the latter species hardly passes out of the Atlantic region. *J. occidentalis* and *J. Californica* are the characteristic species of the mountains bordering and traversing the southern part of the Great Basin and of California. *Cupressus* is wanting to the Atlantic and to the Rocky Mountain floras, but there are three species in the Pacific flora. *Chamæcyparis* is of one species in the Atlantic flora, two in the Pacific, the remainder in Japan. *Thuja* is of two species, one of the Atlantic flora, the other of the Pacific and of Japan. *Libocedrus* is represented by a peculiar species only in the Pacific flora.

TAXODINEÆ.—Of *Taxodium distichum*, in the Atlantic flora; *Sequoia gigantea* and *S. sempervirens*, the Big Trees and Redwoods, in California.

ABIETINEÆ.—Are more numerous in North America than elsewhere. Like the preceding, they prefer the sides to the center of the continent, yet are not wanting to the mountains of the latter. *Pinus* is represented in the Atlantic flora by twelve species; in the Rocky Mountains and those of the Great Basin by six different species, not counting those of Arizona; in the Pacific flora by eleven species, four of which are in the preceding flora. *Larix* has a single Atlantic and two Pacific species, one or both of which occur in the Northern Rocky Mountains. *Picea*, the Spruces, two in the Atlantic, two others in the Rocky Mountain, and two in the Pacific flora, one of the latter a Rocky Mountain species. *Tsuga*, one (Hemlock Spruce) in the Atlantic, and one almost the same in the Pacific flora, which has also the peculiar *T. Pattoniana* or *Williamsonii*. *Pseudotsuga Douglasii*, of the Pacific and the Rocky Mountain flora, most abundant in Oregon. *Abies*, the Firs or Balsam Firs, two in the Atlantic, two in the Rocky Mountain, and four or five in the Pacific flora, one of them common?

CYCADACEÆ.—Being represented only by a *Zamia* on the peninsular part of Florida, are beyond our limit.

The monocotyledonous orders must be more briefly dispatched.

PALMEÆ.—Are represented on the Atlantic coast and north of the Florida peninsula by four species in two genera. Three species in two genera are described in the Botany of California; but two of them are known only beyond the United States boundary; the other belongs properly to the Arizonian flora.

ARACEÆ.—Absent from the whole interior region; represented by seven genera in the Atlantic flora, of which *Peltandra* and *Orontium* are peculiar, and *Symplocarpus*, except that it is reproduced in Japan; on the Pacific coast only a relative of the latter, *Lysichiton*, of which the same species occurs in Japan.

LEMNACEÆ. TYPHACEÆ.—Both nearly the same on the two sides of the continent.

NAIADACEÆ.—In similar case, except that the Pacific coast adds *Lilæa* and *Phyllospadix*.

ALISMACEÆ.—Not dissimilar, except that the Atlantic flora has several species of *Sagittaria* and the Pacific only one, but it has the European type of *Damasonium*.

HYDROCHARIDACEÆ.—The Atlantic flora possesses *Limnobium* and *Vallisneria* as well as *Anacharis;* the Pacific, only *Anacharis;* the intermediate region none.

BURMANNIACEÆ.—Two Atlantic genera and species of South American affinity; none in the western floras.

ORCHIDACEÆ.—Are much fewer in the Pacific flora than in the Atlantic, and are wanting in the intermediate region, except on the mountains, and there in mostly amphigæan species. The Atlantic flora has the peculiar genera *Tipularia* and *Arethusa* (but the latter is in Japan), and some peculiar *Habenariæ;* the Pacific possesses two European genera, *Cephalanthera* and *Epipactis*, but the latter is also in Texas, and an European species of it has recently been detected in the State of New York.

CANNACEÆ.—Two genera and three species in the southern part of the Atlantic flora only.

AMARYLLIDACEÆ.—Are represented in the Atlantic flora by five genera, none of them peculiar, and several species. There are none in the two western floras except *Agave*, and those of Mexican type, and only along the southern border.

HÆMODORACEÆ.—Three genera, all strictly peculiar to the Atlantic States.

BROMELIACEÆ.—*Tillandsia* only along the Atlantic coast; one species north to Virginia; others in Florida and its northern border.

IRIDACEÆ.—Two peculiar genera in the Atlantic flora or its borders, besides *Iris* and *Sisyrinchium*, which are more numerous in the Pacific flora; the former along the mountains between.

DIOSCOREACEÆ.—A single *Dioscorea*, in the Atlantic flora only.

SMILACEÆ.—A dozen species of *Smilax* in the Atlantic flora; one of them barely reaches the Rocky Mountains; a single and peculiar species in California.

ROXBURGHIACEÆ.—*Croomia*, a single species, in the Southern Atlantic States; a close congener in Japan; all other relatives Asiatic.

LILIACEÆ.—Here taken in the extended sense, are largely represented (by twenty-four genera) in the Atlantic flora; are not very few in the

Rocky Mountain region, yet of few genera; and are remarkably developed and diversified in the Pacific flora, which has thirty-three genera, several of them peculiar. Only eleven of the forty North American genera are European, but several of those otherwise peculiar are shared with Eastern Asia, especially the *Melanthieæ*. The characteristic features of the Liliaceous vegetation of the two western floras are given by the endemic genera, *Brodiæa* and relatives, *Leucocrinum*, *Chlorogalum*, *Calochortus*, &c., by *Yucca*, which is also Atlantic, and by the great development of the genus *Allium*, exceeded only in Northern Asia.

JUNCACEÆ.—Are numerous and well distributed over the continent, but require no special remark.

PONTEDERIACEÆ.—Tropical aquatics, except the three genera of the Atlantic flora, one of which (*Schollera*) reappears in its single species on the Pacific coast.

COMMELYNACEÆ.—Also mainly tropical; are represented by two genera and several species in the Atlantic flora; one or two of these barely reach the Rocky Mountains southward; all are absent from the Pacific flora.

XYRIDACEÆ.—*Mayaca*, a South American aquatic, and sixteen species of *Xyris* are characteristic of the Atlantic flora; are wanting to the others.

ERIOCAULONEÆ.—Chiefly Atlantic South American; are of three genera and several species in the Atlantic flora, but none at all western. The remarkable thing is that the most northern *Eriocaulon* has effected a lodgment on the coast of the British Islands.

CYPERACEÆ.—The number of species and genera in the Atlantic flora is nearly double that of the Pacific, and the Rocky Mountain flora has few.

GRAMINEÆ, which would be well worth a particular analysis, are more equally divided, at least as to genera. Of these the western floras have many, chiefly of Texano-Arizonian and Mexican types, which are unknown at the east. The Atlantic flora possesses a few peculiar genera, *Zizania*, *Brachyelytrum*, *Monanthochloa*, *Hydrochloa*, *Ctenium*, *Oryzopsis*, *Graphephorum*, *Diarrhena* (reproduced in Japan?), *Gymnostichum*, *Tripsacum*.

It is hardly worth while to extend this survey into the Cryptogamia, even to the Ferns.

The subjoined tabular view of the Phænogamous orders presents to the eye some of the facts which the preceding pages have brought out as regards respectively their presence or absence or their relative importance in the three floras which we have been comparing. The name in full capitals indicates that the order or group has its headquarters in the flora of that column. Small capitals indicate a full or a notable representation, at least comparatively. The name in ordinary Roman letters indicates a more or less considerable representation; in italic type, a less or scanty representation; the initial with a dash (as N——— in the sixth line), indicates a feeble representation; the blank means that the order is not indigenous to that flora. Thus, the second, third, and fourth orders are not represented, so far as we know, in the Rocky Mountain and the Pacific floras, i. e., they do not extend westward beyond the Atlantic forest region. The next line declares that the order *Berberidaceæ* is, considering the size of the order (in this instance small), richly represented in the Atlantic flora, sparingly in that of the Rocky Mountains (inclusive of the plains on the east and the desert basin on the west), more numerously in that of the Pacific district. *Nymphæaceæ* are in the same case, having very full generic representation in the Atlantic flora but hardly any in that of the Rocky Mountains, and a little more on the Pacific side of the continent. *Sarraceniaceæ* take full capitals in the first column, not that the species or types are numerous, but because the few and remarkable Sarracenias represent the whole order, excepting two species; one of them is in California, and the Pacific column is entered accordingly. Such a presentation is only approximate, but in a general way it tells the story.

| Atlantic Flora. | Rocky Mountain Flora. | Pacific Flora. |
|---|---|---|
| Ranunculaceæ. | Ranunculaceæ. | Ranunculaceæ. |
| MAGNOLIACEÆ. | | |
| Anonaceæ. | | |
| Menispermaceæ. | | |
| BERBERIDACEÆ. | *Berberidaceæ.* | Berberidaceæ. |
| NYMPHÆACEÆ. | N——. | *Nymphæaceæ.* |
| SARRACENIACEÆ. | | *Sarraceniaceæ.* |
| Papaveraceæ. | P——. | PAPAVERACEÆ. |
| Fumariaceæ. | *Fumariaceæ.* | Fumariaceæ. |
| Cruciferæ. | Cruciferæ. | Cruciferæ. |
| Capparidaceæ, CLEOMEÆ. | Capparidaceæ, CLEOMEÆ. | Capparidaceæ, Cleomeæ. |
| Cistaceæ. | | C——. |
| Violaceæ. | *Violaceæ.* | Violaceæ. |
| Polygalaceæ. | P——. | P——. |
| K——. | Krameriaceæ. | K——. |
| | Frankeniaceæ. | Frankeniaceæ. |
| Caryophyllaceæ. | Caryophyllaceæ. | Caryophyllaceæ. |
| ILLECEBRACEÆ. | Illecebraceæ. | *Illecebraceæ.* |
| *Portulacaceæ.* | PORTULACACEÆ. | PORTULACACEÆ. |
| Elatinaceæ. | Elatinaceæ. | Elatinaceæ. |
| HYPERICACEÆ. | | *Hypericaceæ.* |
| Ternstræmiaceæ. | | |
| Malvaceæ. | Malvaceæ. | Malvaceæ. |
| | | Bombaceæ. |
| Tiliaceæ. | | |
| *Linaceæ.* | *Linaceæ.* | Linaceæ. |
| | *Zygophyllaceæ.* | |
| *Geraniaceæ* proper | *Geraniaceæ.* | *Geraniaceæ.* |
| Limnantheæ. | | LIMNANTHEÆ. |
| *Oxalideæ.* | *Oxalideæ.* | *Oxalideæ.* |
| Balsamineæ. | | |
| Rutaceæ. | R—— | R——. |
| CYRILLEÆ. | | |
| Aquifoliaceæ. | | |
| Celastraceæ. | C——. | *Celastraceæ.* |
| Rhamnaceæ. | Rhamnaceæ. | RHAMNACEÆ. |
| VITACEÆ. | V——. | *Vitaceæ.* |
| SAPINDACEÆ. | *Sapindaceæ.* | *Sapindaceæ.* |
| ANACARDIACEÆ. | *Anacardiaceæ.* | Anacardiaceæ. |
| PAPILIONACEÆ. | Papilionaceæ. | PAPILIONACEÆ. |
| Cæsalpineæ. | C——. | C——. |
| Mimoseæ. | *Mimoseæ.* | |
| Chrysobalaneæ. | | |
| Amygdaleæ. | *Amygdaleæ.* | *Amygdaleæ.* |
| Rosaceæ propriæ. | Rosaceæ. | Rosaceæ. |
| Pomeæ. | *Pomeæ.* | *Pomeæ.* |
| CALYCANTHACEÆ. | | Calycanthaceæ. |
| SAXIFRAGACEÆ. | Saxifragaceæ. | SAXIFRAGACEÆ. |
| Crassulaceæ. | *Crassulaceæ.* | Crassulaceæ. |
| Droseraceæ. | D—— | D——. |

| Atlantic Flora. | Rocky Mountain Flora. | Pacific Flora. |
|---|---|---|
| Hamamelideœ. | | |
| Haloragem. | H——. | H——. |
| Melastomaceœ. | | |
| Lythraceœ. | L——. | L——. |
| Onagraceœ. | ONAGRACEÆ. | ONAGRACEÆ. |
| | LOASACEÆ. | Loasaceœ. |
| *Turneraceœ.* | | |
| Passifloraceœ. | | |
| *Cucurbitaceœ.* | *Cucurbitaceœ.* | *Cucurbitaceœ.* |
| *Cactaceœ.* | CACTACEÆ. | Cactaceœ. |
| *Ficoideœ.* | *Ficoideœ.* | F——. |
| Umbelliferœ. | UMBELLIFERÆ. | UMBELLIFERÆ. |
| Araliaceœ. | | *Araliaceœ.* |
| Cornaceœ. | *Cornaceœ.* | Cornaceœ. |
| Caprifoliaceœ. | *Caprifoliaceœ.* | *Caprifoliaceœ.* |
| Rubiaceœ. | *Rubiaceœ.* | *Rubiaceœ.* |
| Valerianaceœ. | *Valerianaceœ.* | Valerianaceœ. |
| Vernoniaceœ. | | |
| Eupatoriaceœ. | *Eupatoriaceœ.* | Eupatoriaceœ. |
| *Asteroideœ.* | *Asteroideœ.* | *Asteroideœ.* |
| *Inuloideœ.* | *Inuloideœ.* | Inuloideœ. |
| Helianthoideœ. | Helianthoideœ. | *Helianthoideœ.* |
| Galinsogeœ. | G——. | G——. |
| | *Madieœ.* | MADIEÆ. |
| Helenioideœ. | HELENIOIDEÆ. | HELENIOIDEÆ. |
| Anthemideœ. | Anthemideœ. | Anthemideœ. |
| Senecionideœ. | Senecionideœ. | Senecionideœ. |
| *Cynaroideœ.* | *Cynaroideœ.* | *Cynaroideœ.* |
| *Mutisiaceœ.* | *Mutisiaceœ.* | M——. |
| Cichoraceœ. | Cichoraceœ. | Cichoraceœ. |
| Lobeliaceœ. | *Lobeliaceœ.* | LOBELIACEÆ. |
| *Campanulaceœ.* | *Campanulaceœ.* | *Campanulaceœ.* |
| VACCINEÆ. | *Vaccineœ.* | *Vaccineœ.* |
| ERICINEÆ. | *Ericineœ.* | Ericineœ. |
| PYROLINEÆ. | *Pyrolineœ.* | *Pyrolineœ.* |
| MONOTROPEÆ. | *Monotropeœ.* | MONOTROPEÆ. |
| | | Lennoaceœ. |
| DIAPENSIACEÆ. | | |
| *Plumbaginaceœ.* | P——. | *Plumbaginaceœ.* |
| Primulaceœ. | Primulaceœ. | *Primulaceœ.* |
| Sapotaceœ. | | |
| Ebenaceœ. | | |
| Styracaceœ. | | S——. |
| Oleaceœ. | O——. | *Oleaceœ.* |
| Apocynaceœ. | *Apocynaceœ.* | *Apocynaceœ.* |
| Asclepiadaceœ. | Asclepiadaceœ. | *Asclepiadaceœ.* |
| *Loganiaceœ.* | | |
| Gentianaceœ. | Gentianaceœ. | Gentianaceœ. |
| Polemoniaceœ. | POLEMONIACEÆ. | POLEMONIACEÆ. |
| *Hydrophyllaceœ.* | HYDROPHYLLACEÆ. | HYDROPHYLLACEÆ. |
| *Borraginaceœ.* | Borraginaceœ. | Borraginaceœ. |
| Convolvulaceœ. | *Convolvulaceœ.* | *Convolvulaceœ.* |
| *Solanaceœ.* | *Solanaceœ.* | *Solanaceœ.* |
| Scrophulariaceœ. | SCROPHULARIACEÆ. | SCROPHULARIACEÆ. |
| Orobanchaceœ. | OROBANCHACEÆ. | Orobanchaceœ. |
| Lentibulaceœ. | I——. | L——. |
| Bignoniaceœ. | B——. | |
| Acanthaceœ. | A——. | A——. |
| Verbenaceœ. | *Verbenaceœ.* | *Verbenaceœ.* |
| Labiatœ. | Labiatœ. | Labiatœ. |
| *Plantaginaceœ.* | *Plantaginaceœ.* | *Plantaginaceœ.* |
| | Nyctaginaceœ. | Nyctaginaceœ. |
| Amarantaceœ. | Amarantaceœ. | *Amarantaceœ.* |
| *Phytolaccaceœ.* | | |
| Polygonaceœ, proper. | POLYGONACEÆ. | POLYGONACEÆ. |
| E——. | ERIOGONEÆ. | ERIOGONEÆ. |
| *Podostemaceœ.* | | |
| Aristolochiaceœ. | | Aristolochiaceœ. |
| Saurureœ. | | Saurureœ. |
| Lauraceœ. | | *Lauraceœ.* |
| *Thymelœaceœ.* | | *Thymelœaceœ.* |
| *Elœagnaceœ.* | Elœagnaceœ. | *Elœagnaceœ.* |
| *Loranthaceœ.* | *Loranthaceœ.* | *Loranthaceœ.* |
| SANTALACEÆ. | *Santalaceœ.* | *Santalaceœ.* |
| *Euphorbiaceœ.* | *Euphorbiaceœ.* | *Euphorbiaceœ.* |
| EMPETRACEÆ. | | |
| *Urticeœ.* | U——. | *Urticeœ.* |
| Ulmaceœ. | U——. | |
| *Cannabineœ.* | *Cannabineœ.* | |
| Moreœ. | | |
| Platanaceœ. | | Platanaceœ. |
| LEITNERIEÆ. | | |
| JUGLANDACEÆ. | | Juglandaceœ. |
| CUPULIFERÆ. | C——. | Cupuliferœ. |

| Atlantic Flora. | Rocky Mountain Flora. | Pacific flora. |
|---|---|---|
| Corylaceæ. | C——. | C——. |
| BETULACEÆ. | *Betulaceæ.* | Betulaceæ. |
| Myricaceæ. |  | *Myricaceæ.* |
| Salicineæ. | *Salicineæ.* | Salicineæ. |
|  | Gnetaceæ. | *Gnetaceæ.* |
| Taxineæ. |  | Taxineæ. |
| Cupressineæ. | *Cupressineæ.* | CUPRESSINEÆ. |
| Taxodineæ. |  | Taxodineæ. |
| Abietineæ. | *Abietineæ.* | ABIETINEÆ. |
| Palmeæ. |  | *Palmeæ.* |
| Araceæ. |  | Araceæ. |
| Lemnaceæ. | L——. | Lemnaceæ. |
| Typhaceæ. | *Typhaceæ.* | Typhaceæ. |
| Alismaceæ. | A——. | Alismaceæ. |
| Hydrocharidaceæ. |  | H——. |
| Burmanniaceæ. |  |  |
| Cannaceæ. |  |  |
| Orchidaceæ. | *Orchidaceæ.* | Orchidaceæ. |
| Amaryllidaceæ. | A——. | A——. |
| Hæmodoraceæ. |  |  |
| Bromeliaceæ. |  |  |
| Iridaceæ. | *Iridaceæ.* | Iridaceæ. |
| Dioscoreaceæ. |  |  |
| Roxburghiaceæ. |  |  |
| Smilaceæ. | S——. | *Smilaceæ.* |
| Liliaceæ. | Liliaceæ. | LILIACEÆ. |
| Juncaceæ. | Juncaceæ. | Juncaceæ. |
| Pontederiaceæ. |  | P——. |
| Xyridaceæ. |  |  |
| Eriocanloneæ. |  |  |
| CYPERACEÆ. | *Cyperaceæ.* | Cyperaceæ. |
| Gramineæ. | Gramineæ. | Gramineæ. |

The groups in this tabulation, it will be observed, have not all the rank of orders. Such as they are, the—

Atlantic flora has ............................................. 156
Rocky Mountain flora (in most extensive sense) ................. 112
Pacific flora ....................................... . ....... 127

But of the groups very slightly represented there is only one in the first, while there are twenty-four in the Rocky Mountain flora and fifteen in the Pacific. If these be omitted the greater diversification of the Atlantic flora will be the more apparent—

Atlantic orders or groups.................................... 155
Rocky Mountain....................................... ........ ..... 88
Pacific ................................................ ............. 112

As to the numerical extent, respectively, of these three great divisions of the United States flora, exactness would be attainable only through much labor; and an approximation is nearly as valuable as would be a close count from present and still changing data. Mann's Catalogue of the Phænogamous Plants of the United States east of the Mississippi, may be taken for the Atlantic flora, excluding for our purpose the introduced species and those of the Florida peninsula. The official Botany of California, mainly by S. Watson, now just completed, includes or mentions the greater part of the Pacific species and genera, but includes many which, though indigenous to that State or near its borders, really pertain only to the flora of the interior basin. Mr. Watson's careful elaboration of the botany of this basin and its borders, presented in his volume (V.) of Clarence King's Explorations and Surveys on the Fortieth Parallel, sums up and analyzes the vegetation of this district; but for the proper Rocky Mountains and the eastern plains no such summary is at hand, although Porter and Coulter's Flora of Colorado has brought together some of the materials.

We may estimate that the Atlantic flora north of the thirtieth parallel (and wholly excluding Texas) consists of 850 Phænogamous genera and 3,400 species; that the Pacific flora as now known does not exceed 620 genera and 3,000 species. Mr. Watson ten years ago had knowledge of 1,235 species in 439 genera (and 84 orders) in the Great Basin and the adjacent Wahsatch and Uinta Mountains. If the ratio of genera and species to orders is the same as in the Atlantic States, the whole Rocky Mountain flora, from its eastern plains to the Sierra, and within the designated parallels of latitude, would contain about 480 genera and 1,930 species; and this is probably not far from the mark.

The botanist will see at a glance the principal contrasts between the Atlantic and Pacific floras. The Atlantic is the region of round-headed and deciduous-leaved trees; the Pacific of spire-shaped, evergreen, Coniferous trees; and the Rocky Mountain forest is of the same type as that of the Pacific, only on a diminished scale, and with the more striking forms left out.

The Atlantic flora has almost three times as many genera and four times as many species of non-Coniferous trees as the Pacific, but it has rather fewer genera and almost one-half fewer species of Coniferous trees than the Pacific.

The forest of the Atlantic States is, with one exception (that of Northeastern Asia), much the most diversified, i. e., the richest in genera and orders, as well as species, of any other temperate region. That of the Pacific is one of the least diversified, except for its *Coniferæ*. Both together are remarkable for the persistence in them of certain peculiar archæological types of the latter, namely, *Taxodium* and *Torreya* on the Atlantic side, *Torreya*, *Libocedrus*, and, above all, *Sequoia*, on the Pacific.

The Atlantic forest is of no inferior grandeur; few parts of the northern hemisphere equal it in the stateliness of its trees, but the grandeur of the Pacific forest growth as to Coniferous trees is wholly unequaled.

These points have been brought out in a discourse by the present writer (entitled Forest Geography and Archæology), which was published in the American Journal of Science and Arts, ser. 3, xvi, 1878, and which, having been prepared in view of this report, it is proposed to append the more important portions of it.

There are certain orders or groups in which the diversification of types and the number of forms in the Pacific flora much surpasses that of the Atlantic, and it is to these that the salient features of the former are mainly to be attributed; and in referring to these, the western interior flora, sharing in these features, may be taken with the Pacific flora proper.

The largest of all the Phænogamous orders, the *Compositæ*, used to be reckoned as constituting a tenth part of the Phænogamous vegetation of the world and an eighth part of that of North America. It forms fully an eighth part of the Atlantic flora. It appears to form between a sixth and a seventh part of the species in the district west of the Rocky Mountains, and a still larger proportion of the genera. Here are found most of the *Helenioideæ* and almost all the *Madieæ*, and of the other tribes there is no lack, except of *Vernoniaceæ*.

The *Scrophulariaceæ* are far more conspicuous and preponderant on the western side of the continent, not so much, if at all, in genera, but vastly in the number of species. This is mainly owing to the wonderful development of certain genera (*Pentstemon*, *Mimulus*, *Castilleia*, *Orthocarpus*), as has been already stated.

The *Polemoniaceæ* form an even more marked feature, the western flora having more genera, indeed five times as many forms and five times as many species as the eastern.

The *Hydrophyllaceæ* are in nearly a similar case; the *Borraginaceæ* approach to it, and so do the *Chenopodiaceæ*.

The *Eriogoneæ*, however, claim the first rank; considering the number of the species and the distribution of the group, no other group of ordinal or subordinal rank is so completely characteristic of Western North American botany as this.

Finally, as to the *Liliaceæ* (in the extended sense), although the Atlantic flora is rich in them, yet the Pacific region considerably surpasses it in the number of genera, and largely surpasses it in the number of species and in the conspicuousness of the flowers.

## III.

### NORTH AMERICAN TYPES IN SOUTH AMERICA.

The botany of the southern part of the eastern great plain of the interior arid district, and of Southern California, merges in that of the Texano-Arizonian belt, and this into that of the Mexican plateau. It is probable that from these plateaux our western regions received the greater part of their present forms and types.

We may expect soon to know more than we now do of the botany of the cooler parts of Mexico, and to have this knowledge in a conveniently available form.

It appears, however, that the Texano-Arizonian species or their representatives do not prevail far down into Mexico, and that the arctic-alpine species and other northern types of the higher mountains are soon replaced southward by andine forms.

There are clear if not very numerous indications that there has at some former time been greater opportunity than now for the extension of North American species and types into the southern hemisphere. And it appears that this has taken place mainly along the western side of the American continent, on which the mountains abut on the coast— that is, as respects American plants which have found their way to extra-tropical South America. On the Atlantic side there appears to have been only a slight commingling of warm-temperate United States plants with the flora of the nearer tropical districts. Thus, the island of Cuba has *Pinus Elliottii (Cubensis), Illicium parviflorum,* some species of *Asimina,* all the *Nymphæaceæ* of the Atlantic flora, *Ascyrum amplexicaule,* &c., our *Ampelopsis* and *Vitis bipinnata, Ilex Dahoon,* a *Rhexia, Oldenlandia glomerata, Houstonia patens, Pterocaulon, Andromeda nitida, Cyrilla, Sabbatia gracilis, Mitreola petiolata, Lachnanthes tinctoria, Mayaca,* &c. These, the *Ampelopsis* excepted, are peculiar to the Atlantic coast. Cuba, moreover, has a species of *Kalmia!*

But more speculative interest arises from the consideration of the North American types, and in many cases the actual species, which reappear beyond the tropic in South America, on the western and not rarely on the eastern side of that continent. There are a number of plants indigenous to Chili, the presence of which in California—where they are seemingly no less indigenous—may be accounted for by the immigration of men and cattle. This may have been the case with *Senebiera, Pentacæna, Acæna trifida, Plectritis (Betkea) samolifolia, Bowlesia lobata, Amblyopappus pusillus, Pectocarya, Lastarriæa,* and the like. For *Erodium cicutarium, Medicago denticulata, Melilotus parviflora, Oligomeris subulata,* and *Arena fatua,* which are now equally at home in California, probably arrived by that route rather than direct from Europe. But we cannot in this way explain the presence in the two temperate zones of plants such as the following, which we assume to be North American species or types dispersed into South America. Some few of them might with equal likelihood be viewed as Chilian types with abnormal northern dispersion. We enumerate only such as come to view without particular search, and exclusive of those which may have been dispersed under man's unconscious agency. Identical species in italics:

*Anemone decapetala.*

*Anemone multifida.*

*Myosurus aristatus.*

*Sisymbrium canescens.*

Vesicaria, said to be *arctica.*

Malvastrum of North American type.

Sphæralcea of North American type.

*Modiola multifida* (Atlantic).

Sida (Pseudo-Malvastrum) sulphurea.

*Elatine Americana.*

Larrea.

Rhus § Lithræa.

*Lupinus microcarpus.*

*Trifolium Macræi.*

*Trifolium microdon.*

*Hosackia subpinnata.*

*Lathyrus maritimus.*

Hoffmanseggia.

*Prosopis (Algarobia) juliflora.*

Prosopis (Strombocarpa) sp. aff.

*Fragaria Chilensis.*

*Lepuropetalon spathulatum* (Atlantic and Chilian).

Gayophytum sp.

Œnothera sp. aff.

Œnothera dentata.

Œnothera cheiranthifolia.

Boisduvalia sp.

Godetia sp.

Mentzelia sp. aff.

*Crantzia lineata.*
*Hydrocotyle ranunculoides,* &c.
Osmorrhiza.
Galium § Relbunium.
Galium § Trichogalium.
*Mikania scandens?*
Gutierrezia.
Grindelia.
Aplopappus.
Nardophyllum (aff. Bigelovia).
Micropus.
Adenocaulon.
Polymnia.
Thelesperma scabiosoides!
*Madia sativa.*
Jaumea linearifolia.
Lasthenia obtusifolia.
Bahia.
Schkuhria.
Blennosperma Chilense.
Actinella sp.
Gaillardia (Cercostylis) (Bonaria).
Soliva (North American species immigrated?).
Centaurea (Plectocephalus) Chilensis.
Microseris pygmæa.
Downingia pusilla.
*Specularia biflora.*
Menodora sp.
*Primula farinosa.*
*Microcala quadrangularis.*

*Erythræa Chilensis.*
*Collomia gracilis,* &c.
*Gilia pusilla.*
Gilia (Navarretia) involucrata.
' Gilia laciniata.
*Phacelia circinata.*
Phacelia (Microgenetes) Cumingii.
Coldenia § Tiquilia.
*Eritrichium fulcrum,* &c.
Amsinckia angustifolia.
*Solanum elæagnifolium.*
*Physalis viscosa.*
*Mimulus luteus.*
Orthocarpus australis.
(Verbena § Glandularia, &c.)
*Plantago Patagonica.*
*Plantago hirtella.*
*Plantago maritima* (Eu. &c.).
Oxybaphus sp.
*Allionia incarnata.*
Spirostachys sp.
*Oxytheca dendroidea.*
Chorizanthe sp.
Lastarreia Chilensis (mentioned above).
Podostemon.
*Lilæa subulata.*
*Scirpus riparius.*
*Scirpus tatora.*
*Hemicarpha subsquarrosa.*
Gramineæ, several.

Here are near upon 90 species or genera, and almost half of them are identical with a few proximately related species. Most of them affect the Chilian side of the continent. One or two are known only on the eastern side. The most remarkable of these are the *Gaillardia* and the *Thelesperma,* of Buenos Ayres; the former closely related to an equally anomalous Texan species; the latter almost identical with a Texano-Nebraskan species. One of the *Strombocarpa* species of *Prosopis,* of the southern end of Texas, is hardly and perhaps not specifically distinguishable from one of Buenos Ayres. Of the 40 or more identical species, only 17 belong to the Atlantic flora; apparently only two of these are peculiar to it as respects North America, namely, the little *Lepuropetalon* of the Atlantic coast, not again met with this side of Chili, and the insignificant *Modiola multifida.* Quite possibly the latter was introduced into North America as a ballast weed.

The natural and obvious line of communication between the botany of the northern and southern temperate zones has been along the central part of North America and Mexico, and along the western part of South America. When our cool temperate flora flourished only along or near the southern borders of the United States, the warm-temperate (to which most of the above-enumerated forms belong) were still further south. When the climate became again warmer, a portion of these plants were as well placed for southward as for northward retreat.

## IV.

### NOTES ON THE SOURCES OF THE NORTH AMERICAN FLORA.

Before yielding the pen to his associate, who will develop the relations of the whole North American flora to those of other parts of the
northern hemisphere, the present writer may sum up, without develop-
ing them, one or two of the probable or plausible inferences or theoretical deductions which the present state of our knowledge, gathered
from a great variety of data, appear to enable us to draw. They are
conclusions the acceptance of which affords at least a clue to the explanation of the condition, constitution, and seeming anomalies of the actual
geographical distribution of the genera and species of our part of the
world. The non-professional reader may best apprehend the ground of
these deductions by a perusal of the discourse already referred to, which
is appended to this report.

The present vegetation of the world is a continuation with successive
modification of that of preceding geological times, and the plants indigenous to any country are completely adapted to its climate, and therefore are capable of enduring its extremes.

Accordingly the explanation of the present assignment of species and
genera is to be sought partly in the geological past, partly in the actual
climate. Questions of the latter kind are comparatively simple. There
is no difficulty in understanding why our Atlantic region was naturally
covered with forest, why the great plains toward the Rocky Mountains
are woodless, and why plains with a saline soil are abandoned to a vegetation resembling that of sea-coasts. There is no insuperable difficulty
in comprehending how high mountains may nourish forests, even when
favored with little absolute rainfall. The difficulty is in ascertaining
how a particular species of tree or other plant came to be a constituent
of a certain flora, at stations widely separated from its nearest relatives,
or even from other members of the same species. This is not a difficulty,
but only a sterile wonder, to those who suppose that facts of this order
have no scientific explanation, or none which they can hope to reach.
It is one only to those who assume that all the members of a species,
and even all the species of a natural genus, were derived at some time
or other from a common stock; but this is the assumption now generally
made in natural history. A reference to the existing state of things will

seldom answer questions of this kind; but a reference to the past may sometimes do so.

Although the vegetable palæontologist goes farther back, the botanist of our era, in the discussion of his problems, may take the Tertiary period for his point of departure. At least, the key to the distribution of the flora of the temperate regions of the northern hemisphere—with which we are concerned—is afforded by the later Tertiary botany.

Our knowledge—fragmentary, yet real—of the flora around us begins with a period when it or its direct ancestors occupied the zone between the arctic circle and the pole, and doubtless several lower degrees of latitude. There it must have flourished until the coming on of that change of climate which culminated in the glacial period. It must at that time have encircled that portion of the earth much as the arctic flora now does. During the period of maximum refrigeration, its northern limits, abutting upon an arctic flora then in low latitude, must have been so far south in the Atlantic States that the vegetation of the northern shore of the Gulf of Mexico probably resembled that of the southern shore of the Gulf of Saint Lawrence now. Of this northern limit there cannot be much doubt; yet we could not hazard an opinion as to where the warm-temperate vegetation of that day merged into the subtropical, as it now does in Southern Texas.

The change between that period and the present, in the opposite direction, has been an amelioration of climate which has carried the arctic flora back to the arctic circle, with which we now associate it, excepting the portions which, in the retreat, have ascended the mountains and persisted there, forming the arctic-alpine vegetation. This, as we have seen, is very scanty in the Atlantic district, where it has abided only on the most northern mountains; while the more elevated ranges of the western part of the continent have afforded ampler refuge.

A similar advance and ensuing retrogression, consequent upon the coming and going out of the Glacial epoch, must have taken place in other parts of the northern hemisphere. Under these great and protracted movements of transference, we suppose that a common flora, which was comparatively homogeneous round the new arctic zone, has been differentiated into the several existing north-temperate floras, and that their common features, and the occasional very unexpected identities or similarities (such as those between Japanese and North American botany) are thus explained. Their respective peculiarities are thought to have resulted from the different vicissitudes and the different climatic conditions to which the primeval stock has been exposed in Asia, Europe, and America, and upon the opposite sides and great interiors of continents, the climates of which—greatly different now—have probably been so from very early times. The plants which were most adapted or adaptable to the one could not be expected to survive in another, or in any other than one of similar or analogous climate. But this is not the place for considering the application of these principles to the botany of the northern hemisphere generally. When they come to be applied to the theoretical elucidation of the great difference between the Atlantic and the Pacific floras it will need to be noted that the two sides of the continent, at the time when they received the progenitors of the present vegetation, were more completely separated than now; that they seem to have been, as it were, two long peninsulas stretching southward from a mainland at the north, the great plains between our eastern district and the Rocky Mountains being then under water.

It may be inferred that the Atlantic side of the continent was more open than the western to the reception of the ancestral flora from the north, and so received it in larger measure and variety, or that it has been since that time more free from disturbance and catastrophe. Probably the two causes may have conspired in the production of the result. There is, moreover, reason to suspect that the recession of the glaciation was earlier on the Atlantic side of the continent than in the more elevated central and Pacific regions; and that, from all these causes, its preglacial flora was more completely restored to it than to that of the Pacific side.

And, finally, we infer that the Pacific region, while preserving through all vicissitudes a moderate number of boreal types, and receiving a few Eastern Asiatic ones probably at a later date, has been mainly replenished from the Mexican plateau, and at a comparatively late period. A large part of the botany of California, still more of Nevada, Utah, and Western Texas, and, yet more, that of Arizona and New Mexico, may be regarded as a northward extension of the botany of the Mexican plateau.

This may, at least, be said: that two types have left their impress upon the North American flora, and that its peculiarities are divided between these two elements. One we may call the *boreal-oriental element*; this prevails at the north, and is especially well represented in the Atlantic flora and in that of Japan and Manchuria; the other is the *Mexican-plateau element*, and this gives its peculiar character to the flora of the whole southwestern part of North America, that of the higher mountains excepted.

---

[From the American Journal of Science and Arts, Vol. XVI, 1878.]

FOREST GEOGRAPHY AND ARCHÆOLOGY.

By Asa Gray.

[A lecture delivered before the Harvard University Natural History Society, April 18, 1878.]

* * * It is the forests of the northern temperate zone which we are to traverse. After taking some note of them in their present condition and relations, we may inquire into their pedigree; and, from a consideration of what and where the component trees have been in days of old, derive some probable explanation of peculiarities which otherwise seem inexplicable.

In speaking of our forests in their present condition, I mean not exactly as they are to-day, but as they were before civilized man had materially interfered with them.

In the district we inhabit such interference is so recent that we have little difficulty in conceiving the conditions which here prevailed, a few generations ago, when the "forest primeval"—described in the first lines of a familiar poem—covered essentially the whole country, from the Gulf of Saint Lawrence and Canada to Florida and Texas, from the Atlantic to beyond the Mississippi. This, our Atlantic forest, is one of the largest and almost the richest of the temperate forests of the world. That is, it comprises a greater diversity of species than any other, except one.

In crossing the country from the Atlantic westward, we leave this forest behind us when we pass the western borders of those organized States which lie along the right bank of the Mississippi. We exchange it for prairies and open plains, wooded only along the water-courses—plains which grow more and more bare and less green as we proceed westward, with only some scattering Cottonwoods (*i. e.* Poplars) on the immediate banks of the traversing rivers, which are themselves far between.

In the Rocky Mountains we come again to forest, but only in narrow lines or patches; and if you travel by the Pacific Railroad you hardly come to any; the eastern and the interior desert plains meet along the comparatively low level of the divide which here is so opportune for the railway; but both north and south of this line the mountains themselves are fairly wooded. Beyond, through all the wide interior basin, and also north and south of it, the numerous mountain chains seem to be as bare as the alkaline plains they traverse, mostly north and south, and the plains bear nothing taller than Sage-brush. But those who reach and climb these mountains find that their ravines and higher recesses nourish no small amount of timber, though the trees themselves are mostly small and always low.

When the western rim of this great basin is reached there is an abrupt change of scene. This rim is formed of the Sierra Nevada. Even its eastern slopes are forest-clad in great measure; while the western bear in some respects the noblest and most remarkable forest of the world—remarkable even for the number of species of overgreen trees occupying a comparatively narrow area, but especially for their wonderful development in size and altitude. Whatever may be claimed for individual Eucalyptus trees in certain sheltered ravines of the southern part of Australia, it is probable that there is no forest to be compared for grandeur with that which stretches, essentially unbroken, though often narrowed and nowhere very wide, from the southern part of the Sierra Nevada in latitude 36° to Puget Sound beyond latitude 49°, and not a little farther.

Descending into the long valley of California, the forest changes, dwindles, and mainly disappears. In the Pacific coast ranges it resumes its sway, with altered features, some of them not less magnificent and of greater beauty. The Redwoods of the coast, for instance, are little less gigantic than the Big-trees of the Sierra Nevada, and far handsomer, and a thousand times more numerous. And several species which are merely or mainly shrubs in the drier Sierra become lordly trees in the moister air of the northerly coast ranges. Through most of California these two Pacific forests are separate; in the northern part of that State they join and form one rich woodland belt, skirting the Pacific, backed by the Cascade Mountains, and extending through British Columbia into our Alaskan Territory.

So we have two forest regions in North America—an Atlantic and a Pacific. They may take these names, for they are dependent upon the oceans which they respectively border. Also we have an intermediate isolated region or isolated lines of forest, flanked on both sides by bare and arid plains—plains which on the eastern side may partly be called *prairies*—on the western, *deserts*.

This mid-region mountain forest is intersected by a transverse belt of arid and alkaline plateau, or eastward of grassy plain—a hundred miles wide from north to south—through which passes the Union Pacific Railroad. This divides the Rocky Mountain forest into a southern and a northern portion. The southern is completely isolated. The northern, in a cooler and less arid region, is larger, broader, more diffused. Trending westward, on and beyond the northern boundary of the United States, it approaches, and here and there unites with, the Pacific forest. Eastward, in northern British territory, it makes a narrow junction with northwestward prolongations of the broad Atlantic forest.

So much for these forests as a whole, their position, their limits. Before we glance at their distinguishing features and component trees, I should here answer the question, why they occupy the positions they do; why so curtailed and separated at the south, so much more diffused at the north, but still so strongly divided into eastern and western? Yet I must not consume time with the rudiments of physical geography and meteorology. It goes without saying that trees are nourished by moisture. They starve with dryness and they starve with cold. A tree is a sensitive thing. With its great spread of foliage, its vast amount of surface which it cannot diminish or change, except by losing that whereby it lives, it is completely and helplessly exposed to every atmospheric change; or at least its resources for adaptation are very limited, and it cannot flee for shelter. But trees are social, and their gregarious habits give a certain mutual support. A tree by itself is doomed, where a forest, once established, is comparatively secure.

Trees vary as widely as do other plants in their constitution; but none can withstand a certain amount of cold and other exposure, nor make head against a certain shortness of summer. Our high northern regions are therefore treeless, and so are the summits of high mountains in lower latitudes. As we ascend them we walk at first under Spruces and Fir-trees or Birches; at 6,000 feet on the White Mountains of New Hampshire, at 11,000 or 12,000 feet on the Colorado Rocky Mountains, we walk through or upon them; sometimes upon dwarfed and depressed individuals of the same species that made the canopy below. These depressed trees retain their hold on life only in virtue of being covered all winter by snow. At still higher altitude the species are wholly different, and for the most part these humble alpine plants of our temperate zone—which we cannot call trees, because they are only a foot or two or a span or two high—are the same as those of the arctic zone, of Northern Labrador, and of Greenland. The arctic and the alpine regions are equally unwooded from cold.

As the opposite extreme, under opposite conditions, look to equatorial America, on the Atlantic side, for the widest and most luxuriant forest-tract in the world, where winter is unknown, and a shower of rain falls almost every afternoon. The size of the Amazon and Orinoco—brimming throughout the year—testifies to the abundance of rain and its equable distribution.

The other side of the Andes, mostly farther south, shows the absolute contrast, in the want of rain and absence of forest; happily it is a narrow tract. The same is true of great tracts either side of the equatorial regions, the only district where great deserts reach the ocean.

It is also true of great continental interiors out of the equatorial belt, except where cloud-compelling mountain chains coerce a certain deposition of moisture from air which could give none to the heated plains below. So the broad interior of our country is forestless from dryness in our latitude, as the high northern zone is forestless from cold.

Regions with distributed rain are naturally forest-clad. Regions with scanty rain, and at one season, are forestless or sparsely wooded, except they have some favoring compensations. Rainless regions are desert.

The Atlantic United States in the zone of variable weather and distributed rains, and with the Gulf of Mexico as a caldron for brewing rain, and no continental expanse between that great caldron and the Pacific, crossed by a prevalent southwest wind in summer, is greatly favored for summer as well as winter rain.

And so this forest region of ours, with annual rainfall of 50 inches on the Lower Mississippi, 52 inches in all the country east of it bordering the Gulf of Mexico, 45 to 41 in all the proper Atlantic district from East Florida to Maine, and the whole region drained by the Ohio—diminished only to 34 inches on the whole Upper Mississippi and Great Lake region—with this amount of rain, fairly distributed over the year, and the greater part not in the winter, our forest is well accounted for.

The narrow district occupied by the Pacific forest has a much more unequal rainfall, more unequal in its different parts, most unequal in the different seasons of the year, very different in the same place in different years.

From the Gulf of Mexico to the Gulf of St. Lawrence the amount of rain decreases moderately and rather regularly from south to north; but, as less is needed in a cold climate, there is enough to nourish forest throughout. On the Pacific coast, from the Gulf of California to Puget Sound, the southerly third has almost no rain at all; the middle portion less than our Atlantic least : the northern third has about our Atlantic average.

Then, New England has about the same amount of rainfall in winter and in summer; Florida and Alabama about one-half more in the three summer than in the three winter months—a fairly equable distribution. But on the Pacific coast there is no summer rain at all, except in the northern portion, and there little. And the winter rain, of forty-four inches on the northern border, diminishes to less than one-half before reaching the Bay of San Francisco; dwindles to twelve, ten, and eight inches on the southern coast, and to four inches before we reach the United States boundary below San Diego.

Taking the whole year together, and confining ourselves to the coast, the average rainfall for the year, from Puget Sound to the border of California, is from eighty inches at the north to seventy at the south, i. e., seventy on the northern edge of California ; thence it diminishes rapidly to thirty-six, twenty (about San Francisco), twelve, and at San Diego to eight inches.

The two rainiest regions of the United States are the Pacific coast north of latitude forty-five, and the northeastern coast and borders of the Gulf of Mexico. But when one is rainy the other is comparatively rainless. For while this Pacific rainy region has only from twelve to two inches of its rain in the summer months, Florida, out of its forty to sixty, has twenty to twenty-six in summer, and only six to ten of it in the winter months.

Again, the diminution of rainfall as we proceed inland from the Atlantic and Gulf shores, is gradual; the expanse that is or was forest-clad is very broad, and we wonder only that it did not extend farther west than it does.

On the other side of the continent, at the north, the district so favored with winter rain is but a narrow strip, between the ocean and the Cascade mountains. East of the latter the amount abruptly declines—for the year from eighty inches to sixteen ; for the winter months, from forty-four and forty to eight and four inches ; for the summer months, from twelve and four to two and one.

So we can understand why the Cascade Mountains abruptly separate dense and tall forest on the west from treelessness on the east. We may conjecture, also, why this North Pacific forest is so magnificent in its development.

Equally, in the rapid decrease of rainfall southward, in its corresponding restriction to one season, in the continuation of the Cascade mountains as the Sierra Nevada, cutting off access of rain to the interior, in the unbroken stretch of coast ranges near the sea, and the consequent small and precarious rainfall in the great interior valley of California, we see reasons why the Californian forest is mainly attenuated southward into two lines—into two files of a narrow but lordly procession, advancing southward along the coast ranges, and along the western flank of the Sierra Nevada, leaving the long valley between comparatively bare of trees.

By the limited and precarious rainfall of California, we may account for the limitations of its forest. But how shall we account for the fact that this district of comparatively little rain produces the largest trees in the world ? Not only produces, alone of all the world, those two peculiar *Big-trees* which excite our special wonder—their extraordinary growth might be some idiosyncracy of a race—but also produces Pines and Fir-trees, whose brethren we know, and whose capabilities we can estimate upon a scale only less gigantic. Evidently there is something here wonderfully favor-

5 G B

able to the development of trees, especially of coniferous trees; and it is not easy to determine what it can be.

Nor, indeed, does the rainfall of the coast of Oregon, great as it is, fully account for the extraordinary development of its forest; for the rain is nearly all in the winter, very little in the summer. Yet here is more timber to the acre than in any other part of North America, or perhaps in any other part of the world. The trees are never so enormous in girth as some of the Californian, but are of equal height— at least on the average—three hundred feet being common, and they stand almost within arms' length of each other.

The explanation of all this may mainly be found in the great climatic differences between the Pacific and the Atlantic sides of the continent; and the explanation of these differences is found in the difference in the winds and the great ocean currents.

The winds are from the ocean to the land all the year round, from northwesterly in summer, southwesterly in winter. And the great Pacific Gulf Stream sweeps toward and along the coast, instead of bearing away from it, as on our Atlantic side.

The winters are mild and short, and are to a great extent a season of growth, instead of suspension of growth as with us. So there is a far longer season available to tree-vegetation than with us, during all of which trees may either grow or accumulate the materials for growth. On our side of the continent and in this latitude, trees use the whole autumn in getting ready for a six-months winter, which is completely lost time.

Finally, as concerns the west coast, the lack of summer rain is made up by the moisture-laden ocean winds, which regularly every summer afternoon wrap the coast ranges of mountains, which these forests affect, with mist and fog. The Redwood, one of the two California Big-trees—the handsomest and far the most abundant and useful—is restricted to these coast-ranges, bathed with soft showers fresh from the ocean all winter, and with fogs and moist ocean air all summer. It is nowhere found beyond the reach of these fogs. South of Monterey, where this summer condensation lessens, and winter rains become precarious, the Redwoods disappear, and the general forest becomes restricted to favorable stations on mountain sides and summits. * * * The whole coast is bordered by a line of mountains, which condense the moisture of the sea-breezes upon their cool slopes and summits. These winds, continuing eastward, descend dry into the valleys, and, warming as they descend, take up moisture instead of dropping any. These valleys, when broad, are sparsely wooded or woodless, except at the north, where summer rain is not very rare.

Beyond stretches the Sierra Nevada, all rainless in summer, except local hail-storms and snowfalls on its higher crests and peaks. Yet its flanks are forest-clad; and, between the levels of 3,000 and 9,000 feet, they bear an ample growth of the largest Coniferous trees known. In favored spots of this forest—and only there—are found those groves of the giant *Sequoia*, near kin of the Redwood of the coast-ranges, whose trunks are from fifty to ninety feet in circumference, and height from two hundred to three hundred and twenty-five feet. And in reaching these wondrous trees you ride through miles of Sugar Pines, Yellow Pines, Spruces, and Firs, of such magnificence in girth and height, that the Big-trees, when reached—astonishing as they are—seem not out of keeping with their surroundings.

I cannot pretend to account for the extreme magnificence of this Sierra Forest. Its rainfall is in winter, and of unknown but large amount. Doubtless most of it is in snow, of which fifty or sixty feet falls in some winters; and—different from the coast and in Oregon, where it falls as rain, and at a temperature which does not suspend vegetable action—here the winter must be complete cessation. But with such great snowfall the supply of moisture to the soil should be abundant and lasting.

Then the Sierra—much loftier than the coast-ranges—rising from 7,000 or 8,000 to 11,000 and 14,000 feet, is refreshed in summer by the winds from the Pacific, from which it takes the last drops of available moisture; and mountains of such altitude, to which moisture from whatever source or direction must necessarily be attracted, are always expected to support forests, at least when not cut off from sea winds by interposed chains of equal altitude. Trees such mountains will have. The only and the real wonder is that the Sierra Nevada should rear such immense trees!

Moreover, we shall see that this forest is rich and superb only in one line; that, beyond one favorite tribe, it is meagre enough. Such for situation, and extent, and surrounding conditions, are the two forests—the Atlantic and Pacific—which are to be compared.

In order to come to this comparison I must refrain from all account of the intervening forest of the Rocky Mountains, only saying, that it is comparatively poor in the size of its trees and the number of species; that few of its species are peculiar, and those mostly in the southern part, and of the Mexican plateau type; that they are common to the mountain-chains which lie between, stretched north and south *en echelon*, all through that arid or desert region of Utah and Nevada, of which the larger part belongs to the Great Basin between the Rocky Mountains and the Sierra Nevada; that most of the Rocky Mountain trees are identical in species with those of the *Pacific* forest, except far north, where a few of our eastern ones are intermingled. I may add that the Rocky Mountains proper get from twelve to twenty inches of rain in the year, mostly in winter snow, some in summer showers.

But the interior mountains get little, and the plains or valleys between them less; the Sierra arresting nearly all the moisture coming from the Pacific, the Rocky Mountains all coming from the Atlantic side.

Forests being my subject, I must not tarry on the woodless plain—on an average 500 miles wide—which lies between what forest there is in the Rocky Mountains and the western border of our eastern wooded region. Why this great sloping plain should be woodless—except where some Cottonwoods and their like mark the course of the traversing rivers—is, on the whole evident enough. Great interior plains in temperate latitudes are always woodless, even when not very arid. This of ours is not arid to the degree that the corresponding regions west of the Rocky Mountains are. The moisture from the Pacific which those would otherwise share, is, as we have seen, arrested on or near the western border, by the coast-ranges and again by the Sierra Nevada; and so the interior (except for the mountains) is all but desert.

On the eastern side of the continent the moisture supplied by the Atlantic and the Gulf of Mexico meets no such obstruction. So the diminution of rainfall is gradual instead of abrupt. But this moisture is spread over a vast surface, and it is naturally bestowed, first and most on the seaboard district, and least on the remote interior. From the Lower Mississippi eastward and northward, including the Ohio River basin, and so to the coast, and up to Nova Scotia, there is an average of forty-seven inches of rain in the year. This diminishes rather steadily westward, especially northwestward, and the western border of the ultra-Mississippian plains gets less than twenty inches.

Indeed, from the great prevalence of westerly and southerly winds, what precipitation of moisture there is on our western plains is not from Atlantic sources, nor much from the Gulf. The rain-chart plainly shows that the water raised from the heated Gulf is mainly carried northward and eastward. It is this which has given us the Atlantic forest region; and it is the limitation of this which bounds that forest at the west. The line on the rain-chart indicating twenty-four inches of annual rain is not far from the line of the western limit of trees, except far north, beyond the Great Lakes, where in the coolness of high latitudes, as in the coolness of mountains, a less amount of rainfall suffices for forest growth.

We see, then, why our great plains grow bare as we proceed from the Mississippi westward; though we wonder why this should take place so soon and so abruptly as it does. But, as already stated, the general course of the wind-bearing rains from the Gulf and beyond is such as to water well the Mississippi Valley and all eastward, but not the district west of it.

It does not altogether follow that, because rain or its equivalent is needed for forest, therefore wherever there is rain enough, forest must needs cover the ground. At least there are some curious exceptions to such a general rule—exceptions both ways. In the Sierra Nevada we are confronted with a stately forest along with a scanty rain-fall, with rain only in the three winter months. All summer long, under those lofty trees, if you stir up the soil you may be choked with dust. On the other hand, the prairies of Iowa and Illinois, which form deep bays or great islands in our own forest-region, are spread under skies which drop more rain than probably ever falls on the slopes of the Sierra Nevada, and give it at all seasons. Under the lesser and brief rains we have the loftiest trees we know; under the more copious and well-dispersed rain, we have prairies, without forests at all.

There is little more to say about the first part of this paradox, and I have not much to say about the other. The cause or origin of our prairies—of the unwooded dis-tricts this side of the Mississippi and Missouri—has been much discussed, and a whole hour would be needed to give a fair account of the different views taken upon this knotty question. The only settled thing about it is that the prairies are not directly owing to a deficiency of rain. That the rain-charts settle, as Professor Whitney well insists.

The prairies which indent or are inclosed in our Atlantic forest-region, and the plains beyond this region, are different things. But, as the one borders—and in Iowa and Nebraska passes into—the other, it may be supposed that common causes have influenced both together, perhaps more than Professor Whitney allows.

He thinks that the extreme fineness and depth of the usual prairie soil will account for the absence of trees; and Mr. Lesquereux equally explains it by the nature of the soil, in a different way. These, and other excellent observers, scout the idea that im-memorial burnings, in autumn and spring, have had any effect. Professor Shaler, from his observations in the border land of Kentucky, thinks that they have—that there are indications there of comparatively recent conversion of oak-openings into prairie, and now—since the burnings are over—of the reconversion of prairie into woodland.

I am disposed, on general considerations, to think that the line of demarcation be-tween our woods and our plains is not where it was drawn by nature. Here, when no physical barrier is interposed between the ground that receives rain enough for forests, and that which receives too little, there must be a debatable border, where comparatively slight causes will turn the scale either way. Difference in soil and difference in exposure will here tell decisively. And along this border, annual burn-ings—for the purpose of increasing and improving buffalo feed—practiced for hun-dreds of years by our nomade predecessors, may have had a very marked effect. I suspect that the irregular border line may have in this way been rendered more irregu-lar, and have been carried farther eastward wherever nature of soil or circumstances of exposure predisposed to it.

It does not follow that trees would re-occupy the land when the operation that de-stroyed them, or kept them down, ceased. The established turf or other occupation of the soil, and the sweeping winds, might prevent that. The difficulty of reforesting bleak New England coasts, which were originally well wooded, is well known. It is equally but probably not more difficult to establish forest on an Iowa prairie, with proper selection of trees.

The difference in the composition of the Atlantic and Pacific forests is not less marked than that of the climate and geographical configuration to which the two are respectively adapted.

With some very notable exceptions the forests of the whole northern hemisphere in the temperate zone (those that we are concerned with) are mainly made up of the same or similar kinds. Not of the same species; for rarely do identical trees occur in any two or more widely separated regions. But all round the world in our zone the woods contain Pines and Firs and Larches, Cypresses and Junipers, Oaks and Birches, Willows and Poplars, Maples and Ashes, and the like. Yet with all these family likenesses throughout, each region has some peculiar features—some trees by which the country may at once be distinguished.

Beginning by a comparison of our Pacific with our Atlantic forest, I need not take the time to enumerate the trees of the latter, as we all may be supposed to know them, and many of the genera will have to be mentioned in drawing the contrast to which I invite your attention. In this you will be impressed most of all, I think, with the fact that the greater part of our familiar trees are "conspicuous by their absence" from the Pacific forest.

For example, it has no Magnolias, no Tulip-tree, no Papaw, no Linden or Basswood, and is very poor in Maples; no Locust-trees—neither Flowering Locust nor Honey Locust—nor any leguminous tree ; no Cherry large enough for a timber-tree, like our wild Black Cherry; no Gum-trees (Nyssa nor Liquidambar), nor Sorrel-tree, nor Kalmia; no Persimmon or Bumelia ; not a Holly ; only one Ash that may be called a timber-tree; no Catalpa or Sassafras; not a single Elm nor Hackberry; not a Mulberry, nor Planer-tree, nor Maclura ; not a Hickory, nor a Beech, nor a true Chestnut, nor a Hornbeam ; barely one Birch-tree, and that only far north, where the differences are less striking. But as to coniferous trees, the only missing type is our Bald Cypress, the so-called Cypress of our southern swamps, and that deficiency is made up by other things.  But as to ordinary trees, if you ask what takes the place in Oregon and California of all these missing kinds, which are familiar on our side of the continent, I must answer, nothing, or nearly nothing.  There is the *Madroña* (Arbutus) instead of our Kalmia (both really trees in some places); and there is the California laurel instead of our southern Red Bay tree.  Nor in any of the genera common to the two does the Pacific forest equal the Atlantic in species.  It has not half as many Maples nor Ashes nor Poplars nor Walnuts nor Birches, and those it has are of smaller size and inferior quality ; it has not half as many Oaks ; and these and the Ashes are of so inferior economical value that (as we are told) a passable wagon-wheel cannot be made of California wood, nor a really good one in Oregon.

This poverty of the western forest in species and types may be exhibited graphically. in a way which cannot fail to strike the eye more impressively than when we say that, whereas the Atlantic forest is composed of 66 genera and 155 species, the Pacific forest has only 31 genera and 78 species. *  In the appended diagrams the short side of the rectangle is proportional to the number of genera, the long side to the number of species.

Now the geographical areas of the two forests are not very different.  From the Gulf of Mexico to the Gulf of Saint Lawrence about twenty degrees of latitude intervene.  From the southern end of California to the peninsula of Alaska there are twenty-eight degrees, and the forest on the coast runs some degrees north of this ; the length may therefore make up for the comparative narrowness of the Pacific forest region. How can so meagre a forest make so imposing a show ?  Surely not by the greater number and size of its individuals, so far as deciduous (or more correctly non-coniferous) trees are concerned ; for on the whole they are inferior to their eastern brethren in size if not in number of individuals.  The reason is that a larger proportion of the genera and species are coniferous trees ; and these being evergreen (except the Larches), of aspiring port and eminently gregarious habit, usually dominate where they occur.  While the East has almost three times as many genera and four times as many species of non-coniferous trees as the West, it has slightly fewer genera and almost one-half fewer species of coniferous trees than the West ; that is, the Atlantic coniferous forest is represented by 11 genera and 25 species: the Pacific by 12 genera

* We take in only timber trees, or such as attain in the most favorable localities to a size which gives them a clear title to the arboreous rank.  The subtropical southern extremity and keys of Florida are excluded.  So also are one or two trees of the Arizonian region, which may touch the evanescent southern borders of the Californian forest.  In counting the coniferous genera, Pinus, Larix, Picea, Abies, and Tsuga are admitted to this rank, but Cupressus and Chamaecyparis are taken as one genus.

and 44 species. This relative preponderance may also be expressed by the diagrams, in which the smaller inclosed rectangles, drawn on the same scale, represent the coniferous portions of these forests.

Indeed, the Pacific forest is made up of conifers, with non-coniferous trees as occasional undergrowth or as scattered individuals, and conspicuous only in valleys or in the sparse tree-growth of plains, on which the oaks at most reproduce the features of the "oak openings" here and there bordering the Mississippi prairie region. Perhaps the most striking contrast between the West and the East, along the latitude usually traversed, is that between the spiry evergreens which the traveller leaves when he quits California, and the familiar woods of various-hued round-headed trees which give him the feeling of home when he reaches the Mississippi. The Atlantic forest is particularly rich in these, and is not meagre in coniferous trees. All the glory of the Pacific forest is in its coniferous trees. Its desperate poverty in other trees appears in the annexed diagram.

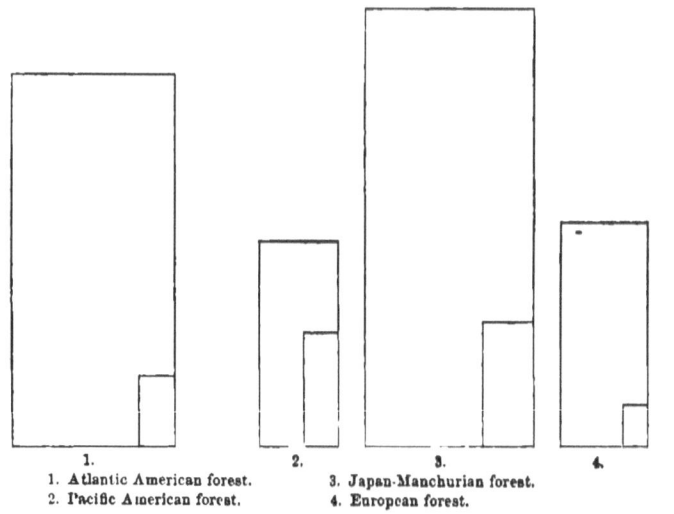

1.
1. Atlantic American forest.
2. Pacific American forest.

2.    3.    4.
3. Japan-Manchurian forest.
4. European forest.

These diagrams are made more instructive, and the relative richness of the forests. round the world in our latitude is most simply exhibited, by adding two or three similar ones. Two will serve, one for Europe, the other for Northeast Asia. A third would be the Himalay-Altaian region, geographically intermediate between the other two as the Arizona-Rocky Mountain district is between our eastern and western. Both are here left out of view, partly for the same, partly for special reasons pertaining to each, which I must not stop to explain. These four marked specimens will simply and clearly exhibit the general facts.

Keeping as nearly as possible to the same scale, we may count the indigenous forest trees of all Europe at 33 genera and 85 species, and those of the Japan-Manchurian region, of very much smaller geographical area, at 66 genera and 168 species. I here include in it only Japan, Eastern Manchuria, and the adjacent borders of China. The known species of trees must be rather roughly determined, but the numbers here given are not exaggerated, and are much more likely to be sensibly increased by further knowledge than are those of any of the other species. Properly to estimate the surpassing richness of this Japan-Manchurian forest, the comparative smallness of geographical area must come in as an important consideration.

To complete the view, let it be noted that the division of these forests into coniferous and non-coniferous is, for the—

|  | Genera. | Species. |
|---|---|---|
| European non-coniferous | 26 | 68 |
| European coniferous | 7 | 17 |
|  | 33 | 85 |
| Japan-Manchurian non-coniferous | 47 | 123 |
| Japan-Manchurian coniferous | 19 | 45 |
|  | 66 | 168 |

In other words, a narrow region in Eastern Asia contains twice as many genera and about twice as many species of indigenous trees as are possessed by all Europe; and as to coniferous trees, the former has more genera than the latter has species, and over twice and a half as many species.

The only question about the relation of these four forest regions, as to their component species, which we can here pause to answer, is to what extent they contain trees of identical species. If we took the shrubs, there would be a small number, if the herbs, a very considerable number, of species common to the two New World and to the two Old World areas, respectively, at least to their northern portions, even after excluding arctic-alpine plants. The same may be said, in its degree, of the North European flora compared with the Atlantic North American, of the Northeast Asiatic compared with the northern part of the Pacific North American, and also in a peculiar way (which I have formerly pointed out, and shall have soon to mention) of the Northeastern Asiatic flora in its relations to the Atlantic North American. But as to the forest trees there is very little community of species. Yet this is not absolutely wanting. The Red Cedar (*Juniperus Virginiana*) among coniferous trees, and *Populus tremuloides* among the deciduous, extend across the American continent specifically unchanged, though hardly developed as forest trees on the Pacific side. There are probably, but not certainly, one or two instances on the northern verge of these two forests. There are as many in which eastern and western species are suggestively similar. The Hemlock-Spruce of the Northern Atlantic States and the Yew of Florida are extremely like corresponding trees of the Pacific forest. Indeed, the Yew-trees of all four regions may come to be regarded as forms of one polymorphous species. The White Birch of Europe and that of Canada and New England are in similar case, and so is the common Chestnut (in America confined to the Atlantic States), which, on the other side of the world, is also represented in Japan. A link in the other direction is seen in one Spruce-tree (called in Oregon Menzies Spruce) which inhabits Northeast Asia, while a peculiar form of it represents the species of the Rocky Mountains.

But now other and more theoretical questions come to be asked, such as these :

Why should our Pacific forest region, which is rich and in some respects unique in coniferous, be so poor in deciduous trees?

Then the two *Big-trees*, Sequoias, as isolated in character as in location—being found only in California, and having no near relatives anywhere—how came California to have them?

Such relatives as the Sequoias have are also local, peculiar, and chiefly of one species to each genus. Only one of them is American, and that solely eastern, the Taxodium of our Atlantic States and the plateau of Mexico. The others are Japanese and Chinese.

Why should trees of six related genera, which will all thrive in Europe, be restricted naturally, one to the eastern side of the American continent, one genus to the western side and very locally, the rest to a small portion of the eastern border of Asia?

Why should coniferous trees most affect and preserve the greatest number of types in these parts of the world?

And why should the Northeast Asian region have, in a comparatively small area, not only most coniferous trees, but a notably larger number of trees altogether than any other part of the northern temperate zone ? Why should its only and near rival be in the antipodes, namely, here in Atlantic North America ? In other words, why should the Pacific and the European forests be so poor in comparison, and why the Pacific poorest of all in deciduous yet rich in coniferous trees ?

The first step toward an explanation of the superior richness in trees of these antipodal regions, is to note some striking similarities of the two, and especially the number of peculiar types which they divide between them. The ultimate conclusion may at length be ventured, that this richness is normal, and that what we really have to explain is the absence of so many forms from Europe on the one hand, from Oregon and California on the other. Let me recall to mind the list of kinds (*i. e.* genera) of trees which enrich our Atlantic forest but are wanting to that of the Pacific. Now almost all these recur, in more or less similar but not identical species, in Japan, North China, &c. Some of them are likewise European, but more are not so. Extending the comparison to shrubs and herbs, it more and more appears that the forms and types which we count as peculiar to our Atlantic region, when we compare them, as we first naturally do, with Europe and with our West, have their close counterparts in Japan and North China ; some in identical species (especially among the herbs), often in strikingly similar ones, not rarely as sole species of peculiar genera or in related generic types. I was a very young botanist when I began to notice this ; and I have from time to time made lists of such instances. Evidences of this remarkable relationship have multiplied year after year, until what was long a wonder has come to be so common that I should now not be greatly surprised if a Sarracenia or a Dionæa, or their like, should turn up in Eastern Asia. Very few of such isolated types remain without counterparts. It is as if Nature, when she had enough species of a genus to go round, dealt them fairly, one at least to each quarter of our zone ; but when she had only two of some peculiar kind gave one to us and the other to Japan, Manchuria, or the Himalayas ; when she had only one, divided these between the two partners on the opposite side of the table. The result, as to the trees, is seen in these four diagrams. As to number of species generally, it cannot be said that Europe and Pacific North America are at all in arrears. But as to trees, either the contrasted regions have been exceptionally favored, or these have been hardly dealt with. There is, as I have intimated, some reason to adopt the latter alternative.

We may take it for granted that the indigenous plants of any country, particularly the trees, have been selected by climate. Whatever other influences or circumstances have been brought to bear upon them, or the trees have brought to bear on each other, no tree could hold its place as a member of any forest or flora which is not adapted to endure even the extremes of the climate of the region or station. But the character of the climate will not explain the remarkable paucity of the trees which compose the indigenous European forest. That is proved by experiment, sufficiently prolonged in certain cases to justify the inference. Probably there is no tree of the northern temperate zone which will not flourish in some part of Europe. Great Britain alone can grow double or treble the number of trees that the Atlantic States can. In all the latter we can grow hardly one tree of the Pacific coast. England supports all of them, and all our Atlantic trees also, and likewise the Japanese and North Siberian species, which do thrive here remarkably in some part of the Atlantic coast, especially the cooler-temperate ones. The poverty of the European sylva is attributable to the absence of our Atlantic American types, to its having no Magnolia, Liriodendron, Asimina, Negundo, no Æsculus, none of that rich assemblage of leguminous trees represented by Locusts, Honey-Locusts, Gymnocladus, and Cladrastis (even its Cercis, which is hardly European, is like the Californian one mainly a shrub) ; no Nyssa, nor Liquidambar ; no Ericaceæ rising to a tree ; no Bumelia, Catalpa, Sassafras, Osage Orange, Hickory, or Walnut ; and as to conifers, no Hemlock Spruce, Arbor-vitæ, Taxodium, nor Torreya. As compared with Northeastern Asia, Europe wants most of these same types, also the Ailantus, Gingko, and a goodly number of coniferous genera. I cannot point to any types tending to make up the deficiency; that is, to any not either in East North America or in Northeast Asia, or in both. Cedrus, the true Cedar, which comes near to it, is only North African and Asian. I need not say that Europe has no Sequoia, and shares no special type with California.

Now the capital fact is that many and perhaps almost all of these genera of trees were well represented in Europe throughout the later Tertiary times. It had not only the same generic types, but in some cases even the same species, or what must pass as such, in the lack of recognizable distinctions between fossil remains and living analogues. Probably the European Miocene forest was about as rich and various as is ours of the present day, and very like it. The Glacial period came and passed, and these types have not survived there, nor returned. Hence the comparative poverty of the existing European sylva, or, at least, the probable explanation of the absence of those kinds of trees which make the characteristic difference.

Why did these trees perish out of Europe, but survive in America and Asia? Before we inquire how Europe lost them, it may be well to ask how it got them. How came these American trees to be in Europe? And among the rest, how came Europe to have Sequoias, now represented only by our two Big-trees of California? It actually possessed two species and more—one so closely answering to the Redwood of the coast ranges, and another so very like the *Sequoia gigantea* of the Sierra Nevada, that, if such fossil twigs with leaves and cones had been exhumed in California instead of Europe, it would confidently be affirmed that we had resurrected the veritable ancestors of our two giant trees. Indeed, so it may probably be. "*Cœlum non animam mutant,*" &c., may be applicable even to such wide wanderings and such vast intervals of time. If the specific essence has not changed, and even if it has suffered some change, genealogical connection is to be inferred in all such cases.

That is, in these days it is taken for granted that individuals of the same species, or with a certain likeness throughout, had a single birthplace and are descended from the same stock, no matter how widely separated they may have been either in space or time, or both. The contrary supposition may be made, and was seriously entertained by some not very long ago. It is even supposable that plants and animals originated where they now are, or where their remains were found. But this is not science—in other words, it is not conformable to what we now know, and is an assertion that scientific explanation is not to be sought.

Furthermore, when species of the same genus are not found almost everywhere, they are usually grouped in one region, as are the Hickories in the Atlantic States, the Asters and Goldenrods in North America and prevailingly on the Atlantic side, the heaths in Western Europe and Africa. From this we are led to the inference that all species closely related to each other have had a common birthplace and origin. So that, when we find individuals of a species or of a group widely out of the range of their fellows we wonder how they got there. When we find the same species all round the hemisphere, we ask how this dispersion came to pass.

Now, a very considerable number of species of herbs and shrubs and a few trees of the temperate zone are found all round the northern hemisphere; many others are found part way round—some in Europe and Eastern Asia, some in Europe and our Atlantic States, many, as I have said, in the Atlantic States and Eastern Asia—fewer (which is curious) common to Pacific States and Eastern Asia, nearer though these countries be.

We may set it down as useless to try to account for this distribution by causes now in operation and opportunities now afforded, i. e., for distribution across oceans by winds and currents and birds. These means play their part in dispersion from place to place, by step after step, but not from continent to continent, except for few things and in a subordinate way.

Fortunately we are not obliged to have recourse to overstrained suppositions of what might possibly have occurred now and then, in the lapse of time, by the chance conveyance of seeds across oceans, or even from one mountain to another. The plants of the top of the White Mountains and of Labrador are mainly the same; but we need not suppose that it is so because birds have carried seeds from the one to the other.

I take it that the true explanation of the whole problem comes from a just general view, and not through piecemeal suppositions of chances. And I am clear that it is to be found by looking to the north, to the state of things at the arctic zone—first, as it now is, and then as it has been.

North of our forest regions comes the zone unwooded from cold—the zone of arctic vegetation. In this, as a rule, the species are the same round the world; as exceptions, some are restricted to a part of the circle.

The polar projection of the earth down to the northern tropic, as here exhibited, shows to the eye—as our maps do not—how all the lands come together into one region, and how natural it may be for the same species, under homogeneous conditions, to spread over it. When we know, moreover, that sea and land have varied greatly since these species existed, we may well believe that any ocean-gaps now in the way of equable distribution may have been bridged over. There is now only one considerable gap.

What would happen if a cold period were to come on from the north, and were very slowly to carry the present arctic climate, or something like it, down far into the temperate zone? Why, just what has happened in the Glacial period, when the refrigeration somehow pushed all these plants before it down to Southern Europe, to Middle Asia, to the middle and southern part of the United States, and, at length receding, left some parts of them stranded on the Pyrenees, the Alps, the Appenines, the Caucasus, on our White and Rocky Mountains, or wherever they could escape the increasing warmth as well by ascending mountains as by receding northward at lower levels. Those that kept together at a low level and made good their retreat form the main body of present arctic vegetation. Those that took to the mountains had their line of retreat cut off, and hold their positions on mountain tops under cover of the frigid climate due to elevation. The conditions of these on different continents or different mountains are similar, but not wholly alike. Some species proved better adapted to one, some to another part of the world. Where less adapted or less adaptable, they have perished; where better adapted they continue, with or without some change, and hence the diversification of alpine plants, as well as the general likeness through all the northern hemisphere.

All this exactly applies to the temperate zone vegetation and to the trees that we are concerned with. The clew was seized when the fossil botany of the high arctic regions came to light; when it was demonstrated that in the times next preceding the Glacial period—in the latest Tertiary—from Spitzbergen and Iceland to Greenland and Kamtschatka a climate like that we now enjoy prevailed, and forests like those of New England and Virginia and of California clothed the land. We infer the climate from the trees, and the trees give sure indications of the climate.

I had divined and published the explanation long before I knew of the fossil plants. These, since made known, render the inference sure, and give us a clear idea of just what the climate was. At the time we speak of, Greenland, Spitzbergen, and our arctic Sea shore had the climate of Pennsylvania and Virginia now. It would take too much time to enumerate the sorts of trees that have been identified by their leaves and fruits in the arctic later Tertiary deposits.

I can only say at large that the same species have been found all round the world; that the richest and most extensive finds are in Greenland; that they comprise most of the sorts which I have spoken of as American trees which once lived in Europe—Magnolias, Sassafras, Hickories, Gum-trees, our identical Southern Cypress (for all we can see of difference), and especially *Sequoias*, not only the two which obviously answer to the two Big-trees, now peculiar to California, but several others; that they equally comprise trees now peculiar to Japan and China, three kinds of Gingko-trees, for instance, one of them not evidently distinguishable from the Japan species, which alone survives; that we have evidence, not merely of Pines and Maples, Poplars, Birches, Lindens, and whatever else characterize the temperate-zone forests of our era, but also of particular species of these, so like those of our own time and country that we may fairly reckon them as the ancestors of several of ours. Long genealogies always deal more or less in conjecture, but we appear to be within the limits of scientific inference when we announce that our existing temperate trees came from the north, and within the bounds of high probability when we claim not a few of them as the originals of present species. Remains of the same plants have been found fossil in our temperate region, as well as in Europe.

Here, then, we have reached a fair answer to the question, how the same or similar species of our trees came to be so dispersed over such widely separated continents. The lands all diverge from a polar centre, and their proximate portions, however different from their present configuration and extent, and however changed at different times, were once the home of those trees, where they flourished in a temperate climate. The cold period which followed, and which doubtless came on by very slow degrees during ages of time, must, long before its culmination, have brought down to our latitudes, with the similar climate, the forest they possess now, or rather the ancestors of it. During this long (and we may believe first) occupancy of Europe and the United States were deposited in pools and shallow waters the cast leaves, fruits, and, occasionally, branches, which are embedded in what are called Miocene Tertiary, or later deposits, most abundant in Europe, from which the American character of the vegetation of the period is inferred. Geologists give the same name to these beds in Greenland and Southern Europe, because they contain the remains of identical and very similar species of plants, and they used to regard them as of the same age, on account of this identity. But in fact this identity is good evidence that they cannot be synchronous. The beds in the lower latitudes must be later, and were forming when Greenland probably had very nearly the climate which it has now.

Wherefore the high, and not the low, latitudes must be assumed as the birth-place of our present flora :* and the present arctic vegetation is best regarded as a derivative of the temperate. This flora, which when circumpolar was as nearly homogeneous round the high latitudes as the arctic vegetation is now, when slowly translated into lower latitudes, would preserve its homogeneousness enough to account for the actual distribution of the same and similar species round the world, and for the original endowment of Europe with what we now call American types. It would also vary or be selected from by the increasing differentiation of climate in the divergent continents, and on their different sides, in a way which might well account for the present diversification. From an early period the system of the winds, the great ocean currents (however they may have oscillated north and south), and the general proportions and features of the continents in our latitude (at least of the American continent) were much the same as now, so that species of plants, ever so little adapted or predisposed to cold winters and hot summers, would abide and be developed on the eastern side of continents, therefore in the Atlantic United States and in Japan and Manchuria: those with preference for milder winters would incline to the western sides; those disposed to tolerate dryness would tend to interiors, or to regions lacking summer rain. So that if the same thousand species were thrust promiscuously into these several districts, and carried slowly onward in the way supposed, they would inevitably be sifted in such a manner that the survival of the fittest for each district might explain the present diversity.

Besides, there are resiftings to take into the account. The glacial period or refrigeration from the north, which at its inception forced the temperate flora into our lati-

---

* This takes for granted, after Nordenskiöld, that there was no preceding Glacial period, as neither paleontology nor the study of arctic sedimentary strata afford any evidence of it. Or if there were any, it was too remote in time to concern the present question.

tude, at its culmination must have carried much or most of it quite beyond. To what extent displaced, and how far superseded by the vegetation which in our day borders the ice, or by ice itself, it is difficult to form more than general conjectures—so different and conflicting are the views of geologists upon the Glacial period. But upon any, or almost any, of these views, it is safe to conclude that temperate vegetation, such as preceded the refrigeration and has now again succeeded it, was either thrust out of Northern Europe and the Northern Atlantic States, or was reduced to precarious existence and diminished forms. It also appears that, on our own continent at least, a milder climate than the present, and a considerable submergence of land, transiently supervened at the north, to which the vegetation must have sensibly responded by a northward movement, from which it afterward receded.

All these vicissitudes must have left their impress upon the actual vegetation, and particularly upon the trees. They furnish probable reason for the loss of American types sustained by Europe.

I conceive that three things have conspired to this loss. First, Europe, hardly extending south of latitude 40°, is all within the limits generally assigned to severe glacial action. Second, its mountains trend east and west, from the Pyrenees to the Carpathians and the Caucasus beyond, near its southern border; and they had glaciers of their own, which must have begun their operations, and poured down the northward flanks, while the plains were still covered with forest on the retreat from the great ice-wave coming from the north. Attacked both on front and rear, much of the forest must have perished then and there. Third, across the line of retreat of those which may have flanked the mountain-ranges, or were stationed south of them, stretched the Mediterranean, an impassable barrier. Some hardy trees may have eked out their existence on the northern shore of the Mediterranean and the Atlantic coast. But we doubt not Taxodium and Sequoias, Magnolias and Liquidambars, and even Hickories and the like were among the missing. Escape by the east, and rehabilitation from that quarter until a very late period, was apparently prevented by the prolongation of the Mediterranean to the Caspian and thence to the Siberian Ocean. If we accept the supposition of Nordenskiöld, that anterior to the Glacial period Europe was "bounded on the south by an ocean extending from the Atlantic over the present deserts of Sahara and Central Asia to the Pacific," all chance of these American types having escaped from or re-entered Europe from the south and east is excluded. Europe may thus be conceived to have been for a time somewhat in the condition in which Greenland is now, and indeed to have been connected with Greenland in this or in earlier times. Such a junction, cutting off access of the Gulf Stream to the polar sea, would, as some think, other things remaining as they are, almost of itself give glaciation to Europe. Greenland may be referred to, by way of comparison, as a country which, having undergone extreme glaciation, bears the marks of it in the extreme poverty of its flora, and in the absence of the plants to which its southern portion, extending six degrees below the arctic circle, might be entitled. It ought to have trees and might support them. But, since destruction by glaciation, no way has been open for their return. Europe fared much better, but suffered in its degree in a similar way.

Turning for a moment to the American continent for a contrast, we find the land unbroken and open down to the tropic, and the mountains running north and south. The trees, when touched on the north by the on-coming refrigeration, had only to move their southern border southward, along an open way, as far as the exigency required; and there was no impediment to their due return. Then the more southern latitude of the United States gave great advantage over Europe. On the Atlantic border proper glaciation was felt only in the northern part, down to about latitude 40°. In the interior of the country, owing doubtless to greater dryness and summer heat, the limit receded greatly northward in the Mississippi Valley, and gave only local glaciers to the Rocky Mountains; and no volcanic outbreaks or violent changes of any kind have here occurred since the types of our present vegetation came to the land. So our lines have been cast in pleasant places, and the goodly heritage of forest trees is one of the consequences.

The still greater richness of Northeast Asia in arboreal vegetation may find explanation in the prevalence of particularly favorable conditions, both ante-glacial and recent. The trees of the Miocene circumpolar forest appear to have found there a secure home; and the Japanese Islands, to which most of these trees belong, must be remarkably adapted to them. The situation of these islands—analogous to that of Great Britain, but with the advantage of lower latitude and greater sunshine—their ample extent north and south, their diversified configuration, their proximity to the great Pacific gulf-stream, by which a vast body of warm water sweeps along their accentuated shores, and the comparatively equable diffusion of rain through out the year, all probably conspire to the preservation and development of an originally ample inheritance.

The case of the Pacific forest is remarkable and paradoxical. It is, as we know, the sole refuge of the most characteristic and wide-spread type of Miocene Coniferae, the Sequoias; it is rich in coniferous types beyond any country except Japan; in its gold-bearing gravels are indications that it possessed, seemingly down to the very beginning of the Glacial period, Magnolias and Beeches, a true Chestnut, Liquidambar, Elms, and other trees now wholly wanting to that side of the continent, though common both to Japan and to Atlantic North America.* Any attempted explanation of this extreme paucity of the usually major constituents of the forest, along with a great development of the minor or coniferous element, would take us quite too far, and would bring us to mere conjectures.

Much may be attributed to late glaciation;† something to the tremendous outpours of lava which, immediately before the period of refrigeration, deeply covered a very large part of the forest area; much to the narrowness of the forest belt, to the want of summer rain, and to the most unequal and precarious distribution of that of winter.

Upon all these topics questions open which we are not prepared to discuss. I have done all that I could hope to do in one lecture if I have distinctly shown that the races of trees, like the races of men, have come down to us through a prehistoric (or prenatural-historic) period; and that the explanation of the present condition is to be sought in the past, and traced in vestiges, and remains, and survivals; that for the vegetable kingdom also there is a veritable archæology.

* See especially, Report on the Fossil Plants of the Auriferous Gravel Deposits of the Sierra Nevada, by L. Lesquereux, Mem. Mus. Comp. Zoölogy, vi, No. 2.—Determination of fossil leaves, &c., such as these, may be relied on to this extent by the general botanist, however wary of specific any many generic identifications. These must be mainly left to the expert in fossil botany.

† Sir Joseph Hooker, in an important lecture delivered to the Royal Institution of Great Britain, April 12, insists much on this.